BOOKS BY

P. M. HUBBARD

Cold Waters	1969
The Country of Again	1968
The Tower	1967
The Holm Oaks	1966
A Hive of Glass	1965
Picture of Millie	1964
Flush as May	1963

COLD WATERS

P. M. HUBBARD

COLD WATERS

NEW YORK

ATHENEUM

1969

Library of Congress catalog card number 69–18794
Published simultaneously in Canada by McClelland and Stewart Ltd.
Manufactured in the United States of America by H. Wolff, New York
Designed by Harry Ford
First Edition

COLD WATERS

CHAPTER 1

Mr. Hastings said, "Yes, well perhaps if Mr. Giffard will do a little more homework on this one, we shall be able to discuss it more intelligently at our next meeting." He looked at me and then round at the members of the committee. He had his Jolly Jack smile on. His face was dark red, and I noticed for the first time that his bird's-egg-blue eyes were very slightly bloodshot. The fact that his questions had been irrelevant did not alter the fact that I ought to have been able to answer them.

At least two other members knew they were irrelevant, but did not say so. Mr. Hastings was in the chair, and he was a bigger fish than they were. In any case, they did not really mind. They liked being on the executive committee. Apart from anything else, it meant that they could come up to London once a month and stay overnight on a cast-iron expense claim. No one knew them in London, and there were things to do in the evening they could not do at home. But mainly it gave them the feeling of usefulness, even of importance, though you had to be a pretty small man to feel like that about the executive committee of the National Association of Platemakers. Anyhow, they liked being on the committee, and if you liked it, you did not argue with Mr. Hastings when he put on his Jolly Jack smile, even if you knew he was being stupid as well as unjust.

Two of them met my eye with little guilty smiles of their own. They knew, all right. The rest were just a double row of faces hovering over briefcases and agenda papers. They were quite blank but not apparently uncomfortable. Some were busy being Jolly Jacks along with Mr. Hastings. There were even one or two I did not think I knew, new faces up for the first time. I should have to get them sorted out presently with Miss Tomlinson from the attendance sheet, but for the moment they were just faces.

I wanted to cry, but was not in the least danger of actually crying. I smiled the close-lipped smile I had acquired at school in dealing with a particular headmaster. I had hated the headmaster a lot more than I could be bothered to hate Mr. Hastings. Mainly I wanted to get away. Out of London for a start, and to a life and job where my inability to remember irrelevant facts about platemaking did not matter.

The meeting ran out on the usual formalities. The last item on the agenda was always to decide the date of the next meeting. Members gave a lot of real thought to this, more than to most of the earlier items. There was a great deal of riffling through businessmen's diaries and rueful head-shaking over suggested dates. It was surprising how heavily committed everyone was. Finally Jolly Jack offered a choice of two dates, and they accepted one by a majority. The losers went on shaking their heads ruefully, but they would be there all right on the day. It was only that for reasons of their own they would have preferred to come to London on another day, but you could not expect them to say so.

They collected their hats and coats and went off down the long corridor chattering in their local voices, Sheffield chattering with Cardiff, Newcastle chattering with London, Birmingham, as usual, chattering with each other. Only Mr. Hastings went off alone. Miss Tomlinson went round gathering up the unwanted papers. She gave me a quick look over her glasses and I gave her the best I could do in the way of a devil-may-care grin. I was, after all, her boss, and she had sat by taking notes while Mr. Hastings took my pants down in public. She knew that I ought not to have laid myself open to it. She also knew, better than most members of the committee, that the whole operation had been unnecessary, and that the main item on the agenda had been shelved because of it. She did not answer my grin, but she shook her head and said, "That Mr. Hastings." It was as open a demonstration of sympathy as office etiquette allowed, and I was grateful for it. All the same, you should not have to be grateful for your staff's sympathy, even the sympathy of an old warrior like Miss Tomlinson. I was halfway back to my room before I remembered the Bottlemakers' dinner.

One of the curiosities of working for a trade association was the program of annual mutual entertainment. It was a perquisite or a cross as you chose to look at it. The way I looked at it varied from time to time—not according to the occasion, because each occasion was exactly like every other, but according to the way I was feeling. Every association had to have its annual celebration, either a luncheon or a dinner. You dragooned your members into buying enough tickets to make the thing financially respectable, and you invited your own guests, who did not have to pay for their meal. The guests included the secretary, or director, or whatever he called himself, of any other trade association which invited you to its dinner. The thing was self-perpetuating, so long as you did not ruin your digestion or lose too many members. It was also quite startlingly monotonous. There were only one or two places in London to cater for a great many associations, and the ritual was as firmly established as the rites of the Church. There was also, for obvious reasons, the same hard core of professional guests. The difficulty was to remember whose dinner it was. Not that that mattered, so long as it was not your own.

I was glad of the Bottlemakers' dinner. It gave me an excuse not to go home, which might involve thinking too many hard and unprofitable thoughts about Mr. Hastings. Also it gave me the chance to get very discreetly, but adequately, drunk at someone else's expense. I have never been able to get drunk on my own, and I should in any case grudge the expense. But if you knew your way around as well as I naturally did, you could get a surprising amount of solid drinking done on these occasions without being too visibly dedicated to this sole purpose. If you did enough drinking before the meal, the meal itself, not to speak of the wine served with it and the speeches that came after it, was hardly noticeable, and this too was desirable, even to the most case-hardened of us. I had my dinner jacket in a suitcase, and as I put it on in the deserted washroom, I achieved a sort of savage festivity. Tomorrow would be awful, but no worse than tomorrow always was. Tonight I was going to get drunk on the Bottlemakers. The washroom had a faintly chemical smell from the liquid detergent over the basins and the stuff the cleaners used in the water closets. The windows did open a bit, but even outside there was only the used London air, which could not make much difference. I took the smell for granted now. It was part of the life I went on living, like my feelings for Mr. Hastings and my headache on Friday nights. I packed my office clothes into the suitcase and looked at my face in the glass over the middle basin.

Even now it did not take very much to make it look pretty dashing. All the mechanics of gaiety were still available, only they needed a pretty sharp outside stimulus to set them going. Whether they gained piquancy from the underlying despair I was in no position to judge. The despair was too real to be traded on. I smiled gaily at myself in the basin mirror and then, after considering the effect for a moment, smiled gaily back. I was all right still. It was the world that was wrong. Give me a new world, and I could charm the birds off the trees. That was all I wanted, a new world. I picked up my suitcase and went downstairs to find a taxi.

The Bottlemakers did me very well. The guests' anteroom was bigger than usual and allowed plenty of room for maneuver. I drifted pleasantly from group to group, always one jump ahead of the man going round with the charged glasses. At some stage later I short-circuited the thing by simply pulling up next to the table where the whisky was. There was a friendly chap on duty, and it was not his whisky. I was looking vaguely for Hallam. He was another sad one, and he knew my Mr. Hastings. I thought I would tell Hallam about the executive committee meeting, making a good story of it, but getting it off my chest all the same. Hallam would say, "The bastard!" and I should get the feeling, for a moment, that I was looking down on Mr. Hastings from a very long way off, even in Hallam's company. Hallam had rimless glasses and the sort of curious tight ringlets that never seem to grow on upper-class heads. I would not choose Hallam for company when I got away to my offshore lighthouse, but at the Bottlemakers' dinner after my committee meeting I could have done with him. I never found him, and to this day do not even know if he was there. The other man found me first.

I had got to the stage where I could see perfectly clearly so long as my eyes were focused right, but I had to re-focus them deliberately for any variation of range, as if they were telescopes. They did not adjust automatically. I straightened up and put my head back, adjusting the focus to give me a long view right across the room. I thought it could not be long now before we were called to the table, and I wanted to see if there was anyone in the room, Hallam apart, I might like to talk to. I found the man watching me. He was one of a group, and seemed to be taking part in the conversation, but it was me he was looking at.

I did not think I had ever seen him before. He had a square, white face, with dark hair cut short and rather heavy brows. He was smiling slightly at the company, but his eyes, fixed on me, were full of thought. I cannot be certain, now, which of us moved, or whether we both did. He said, "Good evening, Mr. Giffard. Letting off steam a bit? I can't say I blame you. Only you won't manage it by yourself, will you?"

I said, "No, I was looking for Hallam." I can see now that this was an odd thing to say, if only because it happened to be true.

He took it in his stride. "I haven't seen him," he said. He stood there looking at me. He was still smiling slightly, but not at my predicament. "Anyhow, you can do better than Hallam," he said. "I don't know—how strongly do you feel about this?"

He was quite gentle about it, with his square, white, massive face only a foot or two from mine. It blurred suddenly, but I felt the choke in my throat before I understood that there were tears in my eyes. My close-lipped smile was no protection against sympathy on top of all that whisky. I gulped a bit and said, "Very strongly indeed. It's nothing new, of course."

He nodded. "Hastings is a bully," he said. "It's pretty nearly his only qualification. It's carried him remarkably well up to a point. But of course the going gets tougher higher up. You're just what he wants. You're better than he is in almost every respect except the curious accident of success. And your defenses aren't more than skin-deep. He knows that, naturally. He hasn't much reasoning capacity, but he's very intelligent. That sort always is." He tipped what was in his glass straight back in one gulp. "What do you want to do?" he said. "I mean, really want?"

I said, "I want to get away."

He nodded and then, after a moment or two, said, "Go on."

I laughed outright into his serious, hardly distinguishable face. I suddenly saw that this was very funny, and that there was nothing to be lost. This chap knew. Well, in a sense everybody knows, but this chap had brought the knowledge to the front of his mind. He was here, at this particular moment and at the Bottlemakers' dinner of all places, standing in front of me and waiting to be told what he already knew.

I could hardly speak for laughing. I said, "Well—you have to have water in between, don't you think? A lighthouse or something. And boats. You know."

He frowned at that. It was not too grave, but slightly disapproving. "Not mucking about in small boats?" he said. He must have raised his voice or perhaps moved his face closer to mine, because suddenly I could hear him very clearly. I was still laughing. "What about an island?" he said.

I reasoned with him. "Well, there'd have to be boats if it was an island," I said. "And they needn't be large boats if it's only offshore. But not mucking about, that's the point, don't you see?"

He nodded, perfectly seriously, as if I had a good point there. He thought for a moment and then said, "It must be offshore, must it? I mean—not really cut off?"

This was the key point. I had stopped laughing now. The thing was immensely serious. "No," I said, "that sounds fine, but I don't think it would do. I just want the thing under control."

He nodded again. I never for a moment doubted that I was making myself perfectly intelligible to him. He was every bit as serious about it as I was. He said, "Yes, I can see that. But doing what? I mean—there's got to be work, hasn't there? Even apart from the question of making a living."

"Obviously," I said. "But something practical would do. Construction. Maintenance. Fetching and carrying. Not cultivation, for choice. It would worry me." He was listening but not looking at me, and I felt a sudden onset of desperation, as if he did not after all believe in what was, to me, so much more real than reality. I did not actually buttonhole him, but I think I must have put my face very close to his, because it suddenly came into sharp focus again, and I could see that even when he was not frowning his eyes were very slightly slanting, like a cat's. They were cat-color, too. I said, "I really am a very useful man, you know. There's not much I can't do." We stared into each other's faces, while the Bottlemakers' party roared into a climax of bonhomie all round us. I waved a hand comprehensively. "Except this," I said, "I'm no good at this. Never have been."

His face receded slightly, but remained reasonably in focus. "No, that's right," he said. "I can see that." He thought about it for quite a long time, and I watched him thinking as if my life depended on his decision. At last he said, "Well, why not?"

"Why not?" I said. Total despair engulfed me suddenly, like a black cloak dropped over my head. I said, "Why not? Why not?" several times under my breath, and through my enveloping wretchedness I could hear the toastmaster uttering his strange hooting cry from the door of the dining room.

The toastmaster was part of the ritual. You bought him along with the catering and the accommodation. He was charged as an extra, of course, but if you did not have him, the Banqueting Manager would certainly look at you askance, and few people can look more askance than a Banqueting Manager dealing with a not very important trade association. Besides, the other trade associations had him. He wore scarlet vestments and used a strange ritual speech which you never heard anywhere else. He was telling us that dinner was served and praying us to be seated. Everyone moved, but reluctantly, and the roar of conversation took on a more subdued note, as if the best part of the evening was over, as indeed it was. People began looking for somewhere to put their empty glasses, and there was the usual last-minute rush of the less confident for the lavatories. Wherever you were dining, the lavatories were always in the opposite direction from the dining room, so that people had to fight their way with a sort of smiling bravado against the main set of the current. I did not want the lavatories. I said, "Why not?" again out loud, and put down my empty glass on one of the many ledges provided by the rococo plasterwork. It fell off with a soft thud on to the deep-pile carpeting, and I stooped and fumbled for it. I put it back on a slightly wider ledge, and this time it stayed in place. I turned round and said, "Because I can't get away," but he was no longer there.

He could not have gone very far in the time. I set off towards the dining room with the rest, but I was looking for him. I was determined to tell him that I could not get away and to make sure he understood my despair, but I did not know what the back of his head looked like and the general movement made focusing very difficult. I even touched a likely-looking pair of shoulders, but they turned the wrong face to me. The man and I smiled vaguely at each other and I apologized as if it was all part of the crush. I found myself seated next to a small pink accountant who was very friendly and communicative. We got on very well, and I could have picked up some useful phrases from him, only my mind was not really on the job.

CHAPTER 2

Miss Tomlinson brought me the draft minutes of the executive committee meeting halfway through the morning. I said, "Oh, thank you," and started to read them straight away. I think she must have thought I wanted to see what she had made of the Hastings episode, because she looked at me a little reproachfully, as if I did not trust her to make a good job of it. But it was the attendance list I was after. I ran my eye down it, looking for names I did not know or could not put a face to. Then I realized that she was standing by, uncertain for once what I wanted her to do. I looked up and found her watching me with a sort of impatient benevolence. She knew I had a hangover. No one with Miss Tomlinson's experience could miss that.

I said, "All right, Miss Tomlinson, I'll give you a buzz— No, half a minute. What about these new people? I ought to know them. Arkwright—who's Arkwright, for a start?"

"Newcastle," she said. "He hasn't been up before. Tall, thin man, small mustache. Didn't say much."

I nodded. It could not be Arkwright. "Oldroyd," I said. "Sounds Yorkshire. He's one of the new Leeds members, isn't he?"

"That's right. He sounds Yorkshire, all right."

"Oh, yes. I think I remember him." Oldroyd was out. I went through them all, sifting Miss Tomlinson's prehensile mind, but I could not be certain. There was a man called Stonham, who came from Southampton and might possibly, from Miss Tomlinson's account of him, fit the blurred face I half remembered. I could not say, "Has he got cat's eyes?", not with her looking at me in the way she already was. There was no one else.

"All right," I said, "I'll run through the draft and give you a buzz. Thank you."

She took herself off and I put my head on my hands. Not that it mattered, after all. I was not worrying about what my man thought. I remembered him well enough to know that nothing he thought could do me any harm. I wanted to see him again as you long to recall a half-remembered dream. That was what, in a sense, he was. Only I knew I had not imagined him. He was somewhere about, knowing more about me than most of the people I knew, but only because he had always known it. And also knowing Mr. Hastings. Knowing him very well, apparently. That might be a pointer. I wondered how many people knew the real Mr. Hastings as well as Jolly Jack. Not so many, from what you heard said about him.

For the moment I gave it up and went to the cupboard for the aspirin bottle. I should no doubt meet him again presently. Only I did not want to meet him unexpectedly and in the wrong place. I did not really want to meet him in company—not the first time, at any rate. I felt certain I should know where I was with him the moment we set eyes on each other. Until then I did not know what to think, and thinking was not likely to do me much good. I took the tablets to the washroom and gulped them down in the horror of unadulterated London tapwater. Then I got down to what I had to do.

Miss Tomlinson had done a beautiful job on the minutes. The reporting was scrupulously accurate, but the chairman's irrelevancies stuck out like a sore thumb. No one in my experience ever read any part of the minutes except the report of what he himself was supposed to have said; but at least the draft ought to keep Mr. Hastings in order. In any case, that was all a month away. My life was suspended between committee meetings. It was like the life of a man suffering from the periodic onsets of a painful disease. The great thing was to get over the last one as quickly as possible and not to start worrying too soon about the next. Next time, after all, it might be less severe. You could always hope. The one thing you could not dodge was the fact that it would happen. So far as that went, the disease was incurable.

I did not have a drink all day and by the evening I was needing one. I dumped my suitcase in the porter's cubby-hole and went round to the Turk's Head, where I always went. There was no more than a drizzle falling, but the streets were wet, and the traffic sounded sticky on the tarmac. I picked my way over the damp in my thin office shoes, wondering, in the inconsequential way I sometimes did, where I had gone wrong and what I could have done to avoid landing myself in a thing like this. I knew the answer, of course, but that did not stop me wondering. Jock Galbraith used to tell me I lacked the cutting edge. He had been a good friend of mine, even if he was my commanding officer. He had had the cutting edge, all right. I had lost track of him after the war, at first in the way you did lose track of people and later because, unless I was very much mistaken, he had made himself, or been made, deliberately inaccessible. I imagined him by now a full-blown spy-catcher with all the accessories and perquisites. As I remembered him, he had had all the qualifications for it, only perhaps too much humanity.

I had written to him, after God knows how many years, only a few months before, using a bank address he had given me when I had last seen him. I had told him where I had landed myself and asked him to tell me what I could do. His reply had come with a London postmark and no address on the paper. It had been characteristic, genuinely considerate but not flattering. I had not kept it, but the gist had been clear enough. He had told me to play safe. I had gone on playing it safe, but people like Mr. Hastings did not make it easy.

The bar was cosy and comfortably full. There was no one I knew. I bought myself a double Scotch with ice and a lot of soda, and it went down like the breath of heaven. I left enough in the glass to look at and sat there on my stool looking at it. It was, after all, the best thing in sight, except for the blonde in the tight black skirt, and she was amply occupied. People came and went, but I did not look at them. I just sat there, looking at my glass and wondering when I need go home.

The man next to me asked me for the siphon, and I pushed it along to him. He was alone. I did not take much notice of him, though it occurred to me afterwards that even at that point something of his placidity and repose came through to me. The weather was getting worse outside. A wind had got up and was flinging the rain against the big single window at the end of the bar. Presently the man said, "Not a nice night for London. I am going to have another drink. May I order one for you?"

It was all done very slowly, with a sort of conscious and deliberate good humor. I turned and had a good look at him. Except that he was pale and dark-haired, there was not the slightest resemblance. The eyes if anything sloped outward towards the temples, as they do in some types of Celtic face. I said, "Thank you very much. I can't say I mind weather much as a rule. Only here one is never dressed for it."

He nodded and ordered two more whiskies. Then he said, "This is not your kind of life?" It was just a question, but it was so near a statement of fact that the thing was touch and go. Like everything else he said, it seemed to come out of a bottomless reservoir of genial assurance. Merely to have him considering me had comfort in it, because he had much more assurance in him than any one person could possibly need for himself.

I said, "No, it's not. But one must live."

He came in very quickly on that, swinging round on his stool to face me. "Ah," he said, "I don't see that." I am not sure whether "Ah" is right. It was not "Oh," and there was a faintly guttural quality to the end of it. Once more there was a Celtic suggestion that went with the eyebrows. "I mean," he said, "you've got to live, I know that. But this can't be the only way of doing it. Not for a man like you." He smiled at me in a friendly, puzzled sort of way, as if he genuinely could not understand my difficulty. Quite suddenly, and for the first time, I felt a touch of panic. I had settled with myself for hopelessness, and could not bear to have my assumption questioned. I do not think it was the old business of clinging to one's chains. It was the mental upset I could not face. I saw myself trying to convince this man, in his absolute assurance, that there was nothing I could do; and underneath my chronic simmering resentment I had no real confidence in my case.

Like most people without much confidence, I went over, rather desperately, to the attack. I said, "What sort of a man do you think I am, then?"

The drinks came then, and we got them to our liking, which in my case meant a lot less soda. All the time he was smiling gently to himself. There was nothing in the least hostile or sinister about it. He was kindness itself. We waved our glasses at each other and drank. He said, "Well—you're Mr. Giffard, aren't you?"

I had known this was coming, but I did not know how. Even the second whisky on my raw nerves had to some extent bridged the cold gap of sanity and disbelief, and I could at least reestablish touch with my mood of the previous evening. All the same, I wanted to know. I said, "Are you Mr. Stonham?"

This was not very carefully considered, because I could not really believe that this man had sat through the committee meeting and that I had wholly failed to recognize him. Nevertheless, it was not altogether lost. He said, "Mr. —? Ah, I see. No, no, my name's Callender, but I've heard you spoken of." The guttural scrape was more pronounced this time. I thought perhaps he knew Mr. Stonham of Southampton, or knew of him, but it did not necessarily follow.

I was far enough gone now to be ready to talk about the thing, but not yet ready to let down all my defenses. "All right," I said, "you tell me. From what you have heard of me, you tell me what I ought to do." I was assured of his benevolence. I must make that clear. There was so little I could do for him, so little anyone could do for him and also so little I could do for anyone, that he must be disinterested. And because of his intrinsic warmth, disinterestedness with him took on a positive character. It was not him I was frightened of.

He put his glass down on the bar with a little bang and turned to face me again, putting his hands on his knees and leaning a little forward. He was full of suppressed gaiety. "Well," he said, "I'd say stop trying to be a gentleman, for a start. You're not qualified for it. I don't mean—" he took one hand off his knee and waved it from side to side, as if he was trying to dispel an offensive suggestion—"I don't mean your manners and so forth. I mean your occupation. The army was all right, I don't doubt. But outside of that, you're not cut out for a middle-class salary earner. If you had any professional qualifications, fine, but you haven't. And you've got no business instincts. You're quite well educated, and you've still got very decent looks, despite the life you lead. You're fit, so far, and you're handy. Now—no one's going to pay you a proper salary on that. That's why you've got into this racket. The last refuge of the unemployable. But you're worth a damned good weekly wage." He made a little interrogative noise. He was still smiling. "I'd pay you one for a start," he said.

I was flooded with a sense of freedom and release so intense that I did not attempt any comment. I simply nodded. Then I swallowed a little whisky to settle my throat and said, "Go on." I remembered that this was what the man with the cat's eyes had said to me at the Bottlemakers' dinner. The whole conversation was developing into a sort of obverse of that earlier conversation. I knew this could not be coincidence, but I could not be bothered to look for an explanation.

Mr. Callender nodded in turn. "Well," he said, "for another thing, I'd say get away from London. Right out, really far. It doesn't suit you. It's not your sort of place."

I knew that sooner or later my turn was coming. We were both still sober, and there was no toastmaster here to break up the conversation. There was no prevaricating with this man, either. I did not even want to prevaricate with him, but I shrank from the mere act of putting the thing into words. This time I did not even say, "Go on." I just sat there staring at him, hoping he would go on talking and not stop and ask questions.

Once more he made that little interrogative noise. It was hardly a question. It gave me, perhaps, the opportunity to say something if I wanted to. When I did not, he made the slightest possible movement of his head and went on again. He said, "And finally, I think you should get away from that place where you're living. What's it called?"

"Ashwood," I said. It had not occurred to me before how much I disliked even the name.

"Ashwood," he said, "that's right. That's no more good to you than London. They go together, of course." He reached out and picked up his glass off the bar. He did it very nearly without looking at it. He was watching me all the time now, and took his eyes off me only just as long as he needed them to get his hand on to his glass without knocking it over. He drank what was left in the glass, quite slowly, savoring it all the way and looking at me over the rim. When he had emptied it, he did not try to put it down again. He just lowered his hand on to his knee and let it rest there, still holding the empty glass. "Well?" he said.

Something which had been in the back of my mind suddenly came to the front. I cannot think why. I suppose it was partly procrastination, but not entirely. "About the army," I said. "I never got my commission, you know."

His eyebrows went up at that. Something surprised him a little, but I could not be sure whether he was surprised at the fact or merely at my telling him. He said, "You're supposed to have come out as a captain."

I shook my head. "Sergeant," I said. "But they never check these applications. I looked like a captain."

"I see." He did not seem any less cheerful. "And I suppose it had to be that kind of job?"

This was it, really. "That's right," I said. "It had to be that kind of job."

"To go with Ashwood and your friends there?"

"My wife's friends there." He was really making it very easy for me.

"That's right," he said. "I can see that. You haven't—I mean, you don't call yourself captain?"

"Good God, no. Only in my application. It's the job that matters."

"Yes, yes. Does your wife know?"

"She knows the facts. Not about my application here, I mean, about my service. Her first husband was a major." I drank what was left in my glass and looked at him with a sort of unwilling defiance. "She's older than I am," I said. "Quite a bit. And she's got money of her own. She—well, I suppose you could say she took a chance on it, marrying me."

He offered no comment on that. Instead he said, "And there's no family?"

"No, no."

He drew in his breath, held it for a moment and then suddenly gave me a really wide smile. It seemed to light up the whole bar. "Well," he said, "that's fine."

"You think so?"

"Oh, surely. There's nothing holding you that I can see. And you'd be a lot happier on Carney."

I smiled back at him, I think for the first time. The whole situation seemed much more under control. I said, "Well, that's for you to judge. Not knowing where or what Carney is, I find it a bit difficult to say."

"Carney?" he said. "Oh, Carney's an island of mine."

Just like that. An island of his. From the way he said it, he might own half an archipelago. "I want a man there," he said. "You can handle a boat."

This was a straight statement of fact. There was no question in it at all. I felt called on to straighten the thing out. "I can't navigate," I said.

"Ah, you'd not be needing navigation. It's not a mariner I'm wanting. But with an island there's got to be boats, obviously."

I had made the same point myself less than twenty-four hours before, and Cat's Eyes had taken it well. I was not disposed to deny it now. "You're perfectly right," I said. "But I don't think I can get away. I've done a lot of building up these last six years. I can't just knock it all down."

He turned away from me and put his glass back on the bar. He did not look at me at all now. I was suddenly left quite alone. It felt very cold. "Ah, well," he said, "it was worth asking you."

He got up and stretched himself. Like everything else he did, it was very deliberate and economical. He nodded, just flicking an eye in my direction. "I'll be getting on, then," he said. "Good night, Mr. Giffard."

He was halfway to the door when I said, "Mr. Callender," and he stopped and turned. "I left my suitcase at the office," I said.

"With what?"

"My dinner jacket."

He laughed outright. I had not heard him laugh before. It went with the rest of him. "Man," he said, "you'll not be wanting a dinner jacket on Carney."

"Not?" I said.

"Never once," he said. "My car's just outside."

I nodded. "I'm coming," I said.

CHAPTER 3

I LOOKED at my watch as the boat went about. I reckoned I could just about do it if Mrs. Callender was not early. Mr. Callender had said she would be at the landing stage at half past eight. I could have simply crossed under power, but I had got up early and found a steady breeze from the north, and the temptation to get sail up had been too strong. It was a great lumbering clinker-built boat with an inboard engine, but you could run up a big gaff mainsail on its stubby mast, and there was a centerboard of sorts. The wind was blowing straight from where I wanted to go, and I could not get within nodding distance of it without nearly stopping the boat. I sloshed backward and forward in a series of short tacks that were little better than reaches, but I was getting perceptibly nearer the north shore, and I was tremendously happy. It was a bright pearl-gray morning, and the air was cool and unbelievably soft. The water under the boat was quite dark. And it was fresh water, that was the extraordinary thing. Miles of this wind-stippled water, with the big hills of the north shore standing up dark over it, and you could drink any of it if you wanted to. It did not seem natural, and I missed the smell of salt, but who was I to complain? The train would have pulled out of Ashwood by this time. I was glad my season ticket was within a week of expiring. It made everything seem more businesslike.

By twenty past the landing stage was clear over my right shoulder on the starboard tack. There was no one on it yet. I came up into the wind and got the mainsail roughly stowed while the ropy little foresail flapped halfheartedly. Then I pulled that down on to the small foredeck, got the centerboard up and started the motor. I headed straight in towards the stage. It was quite high above the water, and the bank fell away behind it. From where I was I could not see the road at all. There was a flight of steps down one side of the stage. There was no tide to contend with, but the level of the water evidently changed quite a bit with the season and weather. I was about fifty yards from the steps when Mrs. Callender came out on to the landing stage. She carried a small case, and someone came from behind her and put another, larger, case down beside her. I did not see him again, whoever he was. She stood there by herself, with the small case still in her hand, and watched me and the boat as we came in.

Even allowing for the height of the stage, she must be a tall woman, probably taller than her husband. And even in that setting and at that distance there was something intrinsically statuesque about her. Under her dark hat and against her dark clothes she looked pale. I thought of her at once as foreign, probably Scandinavian. Then when I was not more than twenty yards out, she reached up and pulled off her hat, and there was a flurry of silver-gilt hair around her face. The whole effect was Valkyrie-like, only the wind was behind her. I do not know why one always sees the Valkyries as beating to windward. They must on occasion have had the wind with them, only perhaps they rode too fast for it to be noticeable. Mrs. Callender's clothes and hair blew out to meet me. They muffled her figure and face, but as I came in under the steps, the flapping skirt opened up breathless lengths of leg and whatever she wore under her skirt. It seemed to me very little. She made no motion to control the situation. She simply stood there holding her small case and looking at me. I tried to meet her eye and keep an eye on the boat as well as looking at what I really wanted to look at. For a few seconds I was very busy.

I made a creditable landing nevertheless, and a moment later she came down the steps and stepped straight on to the boat. She had been in boats before. She put her case down on the floor-boards forward and said, "Good morning. Get the other case, will you? I'll hold her." I might have been a Cunard cabin steward, it was all so direct and impersonal. Only I did not think, even then, that she was that sort of woman. When I came down with the case, which was very heavy, she had cut the engine and was pulling the foresail up. She said, "She'll run faster than she'll motor," which was true. I dumped the heavy case beside the light one and came aft to join her. She had already pushed off from the steps, and the foresail, loosely sheeted, collected enough puffs to pull us out from under the lee of the landing stage. We must have weighed a lot between us. I pulled on the main halyard, easing the boom comfortably to starboard as the sail filled, and we were off. Our progress was stately rather than dramatic, but the whole maneuver had taken no time at all.

Mrs. Callender settled herself comfortably on the starboard side with one casual hand on the tiller. I sat opposite her. Her dark skirt was now gathered sedately round her knees, but however you looked at her, she was a spectacular woman. She said, "Getting settled in?"

"Yes, thank you," I said. She did not call me anything. Mr. Callender called me Giffard, which suited me very well. I did not think she would call me Giffard, and on the whole I had rather she did not. But I did not mind very much what she called me, or whether she called me anything.

25

The great hills were behind us now, and it was all white sky and white water ahead. The island, with its trees and buildings, lay comfortably off the starboard bow, but it lay low. I still found the distances very hard to judge, and I had not yet seen a local map. I suppose it was a mile or something over. I had absolutely nothing to do but look at her. Even if I had been at the helm, I could not have pretended that it needed much concentration. We lumbered steadily along with the breeze just under our port quarter. Presently we should have to do a mild jibe and put the island on the other side of the bows, but it was hardly a matter for agonized calculation. And in any case she had the tiller. So I just sat there opposite her, and generally speaking I looked at her. She looked mainly ahead, but every now and then she turned her face a little and looked at me. It seemed to be a matter of straightforward mutual appraisal. I left it to her to do the talking, and she did not do it. It ought to have been a bit embarrassing, but in fact was not.

I still felt she was a foreigner, though what little I had heard of her English seemed completely standard. It certainly lacked the Celtic overtones of her husband's speech. She was, as I already knew, a tall woman with a lovely body and long legs, but the odd thing was that it was not her body that made her seem statuesque, it was her face. There was not very much expression in it. It was quite surprisingly symmetrical. Very few people have even approximately symmetrical faces. I once read some theory that one side of your face is what you were born with and the other what you have made of it, like hands in the palmist's trade. If that was so, Mrs. Callender must have remained very largely untouched by life. But it was this quite unusual balance that made you think of marble. No sculptor I knew of ever cut the characteristically lopsided face of ordinary humanity. I suppose her extreme pallor helped. She did not lack color, and there was no suggestion of bloodlessness. But there was very little red or brown in the skin, and the hair had a sharp, almost metallic sheen. Even the iris of the eyes was a bright, light gray. She was, she must surely be, a beautiful woman, but she was also, to look at, surprisingly like a work of art. I simply sat there taking her in, and she seemed to find nothing disconcerting in this. I suppose she was used to it.

Then she turned and looked, not at me, but at my clothes, which were suitable, but all quite new. She said, "You've got all you want?"

I said, "Oh, I think so, thank you," because that was what you did automatically reply to a question like that. But it occurred to me, even as I said it, to wonder what I had in fact got and what more I wanted. Already the frontiers were extending. I had lived so long on the borders of tolerability, where even the Bottlemakers' dinner could seem a welcome diversion, that I had almost lost the natural elasticity, particularly, I suppose, of the male mind. Now, just because I found myself in a state of conscious enjoyment, I was already looking for fresh excitements. At this particular moment, leaving aside all reasonable probabilities, I did not have very far to look.

"What about the cottage?" she said. "There's been no one there for some time. I think most of the stuff is there, but you must let me know." She spoke looking ahead this time, without turning her face at all. We were moving with what wind there was, and her hair hung straight round the heavy, beautifully poised head. The profile was straight-cut and very slightly blunt. The mouth looked fuller from the side than it did when seen full-face.

I said again, "I think so. I expect I shall find there are one or two things I want, but I'm doing fine so far."

She nodded, still without turning round. "I'll come down and go over the place with you," she said. "It's time I did. Then we can see what's wanted." She smiled very slightly. "James's decision to bring you was rather sudden," she said.

"Not half as sudden as my decision to come," I said. That at least was true. But what I was really thinking of was the prospect of having this woman, who looked like a Caryatid temporarily off duty, coming round the cottage and checking the eggcups and small forks. There was something intrinsically incompatible in it, but I found the incompatibility very stimulating. All the same, there was nothing wrong with the cottage. I had not found anything dusty or, what was much more likely here, anything moldy. It had been clean, complete, tidy and well aired. If it had really been empty for a long time, it had been very carefully looked after, and I rather wondered who had done the looking after. There was a couple at the house the Callenders lived in. The man was the quiet, rather impenetrable type you expect in a house servant. I had not yet seen the wife. But I had gathered that they came and went with the Callenders. I supposed that was why I was needed.

Apart from the house there were the two cottages. Both were in good order, but one was empty and unfurnished and the other, as I have said, ready for immediate occupation. The couple had been on the island when I got there, and I suppose they could have been working on the cottage while I was on my way north or having my shopping spree at Duncastle. Mr. Callender had given me fifty pounds in fivers and said, "Get what you want." It had seemed a fair amount of money at the moment. We had been driving all night, and I was a bit lightheaded and out of touch with reality. The shops were only just open. I came back to the big car at intervals in the yellow, rather chilly sunlight and put my parcels in the back. Mr. Callender was not there. I did not know what he was doing. By the time I had converted myself fairly thoroughly from a trade-association official into a boatman-handyman, there was very little money left. At precisely this point Mr. Callender reappeared and we drove on.

There was still nearly a day's driving ahead of us, and I suppose he could have sent word then that we were coming. At any rate, the cottage was ready to move into when we got there, and I just moved into it. Everything had the unarguable appositeness of a dream, and in any case I had not the slightest inclination to argue about anything.

There was very little sound anywhere. Half the fascination of sailing is the silence of your motive power, and running before a light breeze is the most silent way of sailing. There was the faintest popple from forward, where our enormously solid bows pushed their way through the ruffled water, but that was about all. Mrs. Callender turned and said, "But I fancy you're used to looking after yourself, aren't you?"

She kept her face turned to me. She was definitely smiling now. I did not think it really suited her kind of mouth, but the effect was very disturbing. Once those curved, chiseled lips softened at all, your mind ran riot on what they would do and look like with the blood in them and the breath forced out between them. I smiled back at her, but my mind was busy on its secret picture of her. There was still this curious gap between what I saw and my experience of her as a person.

"I wouldn't say I'm used to it," I said. "I like it, all right. It's a bit of a luxury, to tell the truth."

"I see, yes. I won't interfere, I promise."

"As a matter of fact, I don't think you will," I said, this being, as it happened, what I thought. Then, because she was still smiling at me and there was nothing to lose anyway, I said, "But do please try."

Her mouth twitched, so that for a moment she looked almost mischievous. But she shook her head and turned back to her steering. That was all we said until she decided, at the very moment I had decided myself, that it was time to put our head round. Then she just said, "Jibing," and I nodded and caught the heavy boom as it swung over and let it run out easily on my side of the boat.

The island had a small stone jetty built out from the rocks on its northern side. The prevailing wind, and I imagined all the hard blows, came from the west, and the jetty had a sandy beach east of it. It was as near a harbor as you needed in non-tidal waters. We had gone over so far eastward that now we were almost reaching across the wind, pointing straight for the end of the jetty. At the last moment she simply turned offwind, let the sheet go and ran straight up on to the beach. The centerboard was already up. It was all extremely simple but perfectly efficient. She was still, after all, wearing her dark town clothes and had her little black hat in her lap. We were not out for a sail. We were simply getting home. She waited till the boat had settled. Then she got up, walked forward and jumped on to the sand. Her black shoes were still quite dry. I handed her small case out to her and said, "I'll bring the other one up." She nodded and walked up the beach to the path at the shore end of the jetty. Even in the soft sand her stride was almost as long as mine.

For a moment or two I did unnecessary things with my hands while I watched her go up the path. Then I got the sails down and stowed, lugged the lightened boat a few more feet up the sand and made her fast to a stake driven into the dark, rocky soil above the beach. I stood there looking her over. There were various small things I thought I could do to make her handier and more comfortable, and the paint needed attention inside and out. She would never be a racer, but she had been built for these waters and I was already very fond of her. I thought of Cat's Eyes saying, "Not mucking about in small boats?" and cocked a mental snoot at him. As I had said at the time, there had to be boats, and any boat needs attention. I picked up the big case and set off up the path. I had gone no distance at all when I began to wonder what the case held. If it was only clothes, they must be pretty densely packed. My muscles were beginning to feel in much better shape than they had been, and I had regained a little of my old pride and interest in my mere physical ability. Even so, I had to change the case from one hand to the other as I went up the hill. Ultimately, at a place where I was out of sight of the house, I put the case down and rested. I told myself I did not want to get into a sweat at this time of the morning. In fact I was out of breath and my arms and shoulders ached. I was a long way off a proper condition yet.

I picked up the case and went up over the brow of the slope. I passed the two cottages and walked on, with a determined freedom of stride, towards the stone terrace of the house.

CHAPTER 4

I DID NOT THINK it could ever have been a working house, because there was nothing to work. The island was not more than a few hundred yards long from east to west and less the other way. It was too far from the shore to control any of the land there with any sort of convenience, and the house looked as if it had been built long after the time when, even in these parts, private defense had been a consideration. Someone had built it for his pleasure, because he fancied living on an island and probably enjoyed fishing. It was solid stone, low-built and slated. The stone had come out of the western end of the island. The quarry was overgrown now except for the walls, but you could still, in your mind's eye, fit the house, block by block, into it. I thought it was not more than a hundred years old at the outside. They made their own electricity. The powerhouse was on the south side, right over the water, with a small winch for picking up the oil drums out of the boat. There was a rowing boat for the fishing, and no doubt an outboard if you wanted it, but mine was the cargo ship of the establishment. I did not seem to be responsible for the power plant, but it would evidently be up to me to keep it fueled. It was a place after my own heart, except that I should have liked salt water.

The man came out of the side door of the house when I was halfway across the terrace. I hadn't got his name. Mr. Callender had mentioned it, but I was bad at names, and it was nothing very memorable. It didn't seem to matter very much, because he was not the sort of man who needed any very positive identification. I would make sure of it next time Mr. Callender mentioned it. For the moment he merely held out his hand for the case and said, "Right, I'll take that." I was already quite glad to be rid of it, but I noticed that he did not seem to make much of a burden of it, though he was a smallish chap. I had turned to go down to the cottage when Mr. Callender called to me from the front door.

Either he had not changed his style of dress as much as I had, or he was a man clothes made very little difference to. He still looked very much as he had when I first saw him. I think it was a bit of both. I could not imagine him in jeans and a roll-necked jersey, even here. He was changed, for me, not because of any difference in himself, but because I now knew he had the wife he had. He was not the first man I had known changed in this way. You could not help speculating on the relation between them, when there were such reserves of strength on both sides. In so far as his relation with me had changed, the change was all on my side. His warmth and assurance were as unchanged as his style of dress, and in some way went with it.

He said, "You've been out under sail, I hear?" He knew exactly what this meant to me, and seemed pleased by it. There was nothing for me to explain. I nodded, and we stood there smiling at each other.

"Any second thoughts?"

"Not so far."

"Any word to the south?"

"I don't think so."

"I think you're wise. But let me know if you change your mind."

"I will. But I don't think I shall."

"Good. Come up in about an hour's time, will you? Then we'll go round and see what there is for you to do. And about supplies and so on."

All the time he was speaking I was conscious of Mrs. Callender in the house behind him. I have no idea where in the house she was. I could not see her and had no reason whatever to think she could see me. But the fact that she was there underlay the whole situation. Some sort of a direct link, however tenuous, between myself and her already existed and Mr. Callender, standing smiling in the doorway, cut across it. And yet I knew him, and as far as I could tell liked him very much, whereas I knew her hardly at all and did not particularly like what I knew. I walked back down the path to the cottage, smelling the sweet, damp air and full of a wholly uncritical elation.

My kitchen window faced north. I washed up the breakfast things looking out over the short slope of the island and a mile or so of flat water at the big hills beyond it. I was just mopping down the draining board when, somewhere over my right shoulder, the sun broke out of the cloudbank and the air changed color. The sky and hills to the north were still gray, and the water took its color from them, but the gray was overlaid with a sort of golden wash where the sunlight caught the vapor over its surface. With the wind gone, we looked set for a fine day. Nothing I could see moved, and it was completely quiet.

The window was open. I heard the footsteps coming round from the front of the cottage and at once thought of Mrs. Callender, because that was the way my mind was working. She had, after all, said she would come. The woman who suddenly appeared outside the window could hardly have been less like her. To begin with, she was short. The gravel outside was in any case below the level of the kitchen floor, and what with this and her shortness, we found ourselves peering at each other between the hot and cold taps of the sink. She seemed as startled as I was. I could not think why, when she had presumably come looking for me. She had a plump, hour-glass figure, an elaborate mass of very dark hair and big green eyes which at the moment looked almost completely round. She wore a very short black dress ruthlessly taken in everywhere it could be taken in. She looked for all the world like the flighty French maid in old-fashioned farce. Her lips were bunched up as if she was going to whistle, and when she got her breath she said, "Oooh."

I hope it was not rude of me, but I burst out laughing. It was at least partly surprise. I had certainly as much right to be surprised as she had. Of course, I was laughing at her, but there was no derision in it. Her whole style and appearance were wildly incongruous against that vast, empty landscape, but on any count she was a sight for sore eyes, even if her appeal tended towards the universal.

She said, "You're Mr. Giffard?" She stressed the you, as if she knew there had to be a Mr. Giffard, but could not believe I was it. As she could almost certainly see little more than my head and neck, it must be there her difficulty lay. I wondered whether anyone had told her I was a Negro or Chinese or something equally distinctive.

I said, "Yes, come in." There was a door opening direct from the kitchen to the northern side of the cottage, and I went and opened it. By this time she had come back from the window and was standing directly under the couple of steps that went down from the door. I stood on top of the steps looking down at her and she stood on the gravel looking up at me. I had taken off my jersey and was wearing a working shirt and corduroys. A fine manly figure, even if my muscles were not yet in all that good shape. She looked more ooh-la-la than ever. She stared at me as if I were Steve Reeves or Errol Flynn or whatever it was she fancied. I said again, "Come in," and stood back from the top step.

She came up the steps and into the kitchen with the most emphatic circumspection, as if she did not know what she was letting herself in for. When she was inside, she ran her big green eyes all round the room, giving me a quick look between one wall and the next. As I imagined she must have cleaned the place up thoroughly not so long ago, I wondered what she expected to see. From the look of her, it might be anything from a bloodstained hatchet to obscene photographs. I was on the point of asking her if she would like to see my etchings when she found her voice. She said, "Mr. Callender says can you come up in five minutes, because he's got to go off earlier than he expected."

I had not, of course, known that Mr. Callender was going off at all. What I immediately wanted to know was whether Mrs. Callender was going too. I looked at Fifi with the question on the tip of my tongue, but decided against it. I should know soon enough in any case and, even as between servants, I had the man's instinct not to do anything to suggest to one woman my interest in another. I said, "Right, I'll be up."

She had finished inspecting the room and was now looking at me again, pouting a little. She did everything in character. She said, "Why did you laugh just now?"

I smiled into her outraged eyes and after a moment she gave me a hesitant half-smile in return. She really was rather taking. "I'm sorry," I said, "you startled me. I hadn't seen you before, and to tell the truth you were a bit unexpected. In a place like this, I mean."

It sounded a bit lame, but I thought I could give it a suitable twist if she gave me the right opening. She did, bless her. She said, "Don't I look right, then?" If there had been a glass in the room, she would have looked herself over in it. As there was not, she looked herself over direct, as far as she could. She even put a hand up to her hair, to make sure it was all in order.

"You look wonderful," I said, and meant it. "But you aren't the sort of person one expects to meet in a place like this. Well —do you think you are?"

She was pleased, of course. She gave me a proper smile. "Perhaps not," she said.

"Anyway," I said, "the next time you come and see me, I promise you I won't laugh."

She looked thoroughly alarmed. She said, "Next time? Oh, I don't know—" She said it as if I had already suggested a weekend at Brighton, or whatever the local equivalent was. Her mind was still a couple of jumps ahead of me, but I was beginning to catch up. However obvious her attractions were, they were very real, and in my sunlit, after-breakfast mood they appealed to me immediately and powerfully. I was not over-concerned with matters of taste. But for the moment the great thing was to make everything outwardly friendly and respectable. I could rely on her not to miss the undercurrents.

"Well," I said, "you'll come and give me a hand sometimes, won't you? Just to keep the place straight. I'm only a man, you know." Coming from a man who would not, from experience and conviction, trust a woman even to wash a teacup properly, this was fairly deliberate dishonesty. I wished I had got the place less tidy than I had. But it served. She was looking for a rationalization as much as I was, only in her case I think it was instinctive and not deliberate. She at once looked less alarmed, and her natural friendliness reasserted itself.

She said, "Oh, I expect I could come down and do a bit of cleaning sometimes. That's if you wanted me."

"I'd want you," I said. Perhaps I put a shade too much meaning into it, because she opened her eyes wide at me. I gave her a cheerful, friendly smile, daring her to see any harm in the thing, and she tossed her dark head. I do not think I had ever actually seen anyone toss her head before. I had only read about it in period books. But that, clearly, was what she did.

"We'll see," she said. She turned and went slowly towards the door, and I watched every muscle move under the shiny black stuff of her dress. There was a single zip running from the back of her neck to well below the line of her hips, and I was desperate to know what would happen when the pressure system was released. But of course I just stood there and watched her go. I did not move until she was safely down the steps. Then I went and stood in the doorway, looking down at her as I had at first.

"Anyway," I said, "thank you for coming. I'll be up in five minutes. Will you tell Mr. Callender?"

"I'll tell him," she said. She went off over the gravel, stepping carefully in her pressurized skirt, but I didn't wait to see her go. I presented myself at the house four and a half minutes later.

The small man—I still did not know his name—had taken on a fresh interest, as Mr. Callender himself had, once I had seen his wife. Unless I was letting the excitement of my new life run away with my judgment, being married to Fifi must have its highly pleasurable side, but it could not be without its stresses. He appeared when I knocked at the side door. There was nothing to suggest that my recent interview with his wife had increased his interest in me as it had mine in him. He just nodded and said, "I'll tell Mr. Callender you're here." I could not swear to his voice, any more than I could to Fifi's. Couples in domestic service these days are seldom natives, but I could not begin to place this one with any particular nationality. Their English was perfect and of their class, allowing for the flattening effect of domestic service on behavior and speech. As with Mrs. Callender, I found myself thinking of them both as foreign, but could not, on reflection, find any reason why I should. I was still thinking about it when Mr. Callender came round from the front of the house.

He said, "Come to the front door if you want me. There's no need to bother George. We don't have carriage visitors, after all."

"Right," I said, "I will. George's name, by the way—I think you did tell me, but I didn't take it in."

"Benson. But I expect when you know them well enough, you'll be calling them George and Carrie, as we do."

Carrie, I thought. Not Fifi quite, but near enough. I said, "Yes, of course. But I thought I'd better get it right."

"Quite right. Now—where do we start?"

They owned the island and a piece of the north shore opposite, where the landing stage was. There was a gate on the main road and then a private road across what I took to be open moor. The garage was just inshore from the landing stage, but down under the high ground of the bank, so that you could not see it from the water. It was a solid job of stone with steel doors. It had to be, I suppose. It was very much on its own, and anyone could come in from the road. There was no garden to the house, only terraced lawn and a few flower beds under the walls. The grass was my job, but Mrs. Callender and Fifi did the flowers. Even the vegetables came by water. The whole domestic economy hung on the deep freeze, and the deep freeze, of course, hung on the power supply. "There's a spare motor for emergencies," Mr. Callender said. "We can't afford a power cut. George looks after the plant. That won't be your responsibility at all." He seemed to consider this for a moment. "At least," he said, "I don't think George will want you to help there, but you'd better fall in with whatever he wants. That's his department."

"I will," I said. The rest was routine maintenance stuff, buildings, boats and equipment generally. There was no lessening of the geniality, but Mr. Callender explained exactly what he wanted and made it clear that he expected to get it. I liked this very much. After the shadow-boxing and showmanship of the last few years I had a job to do and knew I could do it.

We walked back to the house in silence, but just before we got there he said, "Happy?"

I felt suddenly emotional about it all, so emotional that all I said was "Yes."

"Why, in particular?"

I thought about this. We had come up on to the terrace in front of the house and stood there in the huge sunlit silence while I thought. "I think," I said, "because I have got to do the work myself."

"You don't like giving orders?"

"Not much. I was once told I was a top-class subordinate."

He smiled. "Who told you that?"

"A man called Galbraith."

"He knew what he was talking about?"

"Oh, yes. He had every reason to know."

"This was in your army days?"

"That's right. He was my commanding officer, as a matter of fact, but it was a pretty odd set-up."

"Odd how?" he said.

"Well—what you might call paramilitary. One of these intelligence things."

He smiled quite broadly at that. There was no mockery in it, but the improbability of it seemed to strike him, as it sometimes had me. "Cloak-and-dagger stuff?" he said.

"Not me. The nearest I got to a dagger was a paperknife. But I knew those who were, of course."

He nodded and looked at his watch. "I want to go across in about twenty minutes," he said. "I think we'll motor, if you don't mind."

I looked across the sheet of shining water. The sea is never motionless, but here nothing stirred at all. "I'm sure you're right," I said.

CHAPTER 5

I LEFT THE BOAT on the beach and walked up the path, wondering what to do first. I wanted, quite simply, to do something near the house, where I might get a sight of Mrs. Callender. I decided on the terrace grass. It needed cutting, and anything that grows can always stake a claim for prior attention. I came to my cottage, considered whether there was anything to go in for, decided there was not and went on to the empty cottage just above it. The two were exactly alike. Further south they would have been built as a semi-detached pair. I was glad they had not been. I saw no reason to think that the other would at any time be occupied, but in a place like this I did not like the idea of living in a piece with another house, even if it was empty. I turned off the path, walked across the gravel and peered in through the uncurtained windows. There was no furniture to be seen, but even the decorations were the same.

I turned to go on up the path and then, as something in my mind buzzed faintly for attention, turned again and went back to the window. It was the sitting room I was looking at. The sun streamed past me, striking full on the paintwork of the opposite wall. The thing that had caught my eye really was there. The wall was a pale green, and in two places there were rectangles of very slightly darker green, where something had stood against the wall and protected the paintwork from the light. I knew now what it was that had struck me. In my own cottage that wall of the sitting room had two pieces of furniture against it, a small writing table and a set of shelves. Unless I was mistaken, they would fit the darker patches on the wall I was looking at. The cottages were not only similarly decorated. They had apparently at one time been exactly similarly furnished.

It did not matter in the least, but I wanted to see if I was right. I went down to my own cottage, went through the front door into the tiny hall and turned left into the sitting room. There were the writing table and shelves, almost exactly as I had remembered them. They were just the right size and shape. The windows here were curtained, but even so the sun streamed in and lit up the undistinguished woodwork. It was the most ordinary modern furniture, quite solid but mass-produced. I wondered why its counterparts had been taken out of the empty cottage and where they had gone. I was pleased in a mild way with my observation, but it was not a thing to exercise my mind over. I made for the door and then, for the second time that morning, turned as a thought struck me and went back to the writing table. I moved it slightly away from the wall and looked behind it. There was no mark at all. The whole wall was of a uniform color.

I knew now where the furniture from the other cottage had gone. It had come here. This had been the empty cottage. At some point and for some reason the furniture had been moved out of the other cottage and put in the corresponding places here. I wondered, of course, whether it had been done against my arrival. I could think of no reason why anyone should, but it looked as if someone had decided that I should occupy the lower cottage and not the upper one, although at the time it was the upper one that was furnished. My predecessor, if I had had a predecessor, had presumably lived there. I say I could think of no reason for this, but of course any number of explanations, all equally speculative, occurred to me. I think if anything I came down in favor of the belief that it had something to do with moving me further away from the house and putting the empty cottage between me and it. I suppose I connected this in some irrational way with my interest in Mrs. Callender. But it was no more than idle thinking. There was no reason why I should take the thing seriously, and I did not. I put the writing table back against the bleached paintwork and went back into the hall. I had left the front door open when I came in. As I came into the hall, I saw Mrs. Callender turn off the path and come towards me.

My immediate impression was that she had nothing on below the waist, but the illusion did not last very long. Apart from the intrinsic probabilities, the uncovered human body is never as smooth and tidy as that. She had on some sort of very close-fitting trousers. I am not an expert on materials, but the stuff was soft and elastic enough to mold itself very closely to the skin beneath it, but was not in fact very thin and certainly not to any degree transparent. The surface was matt and the color near enough skin color to be momentarily startling, but as a garment the thing was entirely decent. It had none of the suggestiveness of Fifi's flounces. It merely proclaimed, what I already knew, that Mrs. Callender was a magnificently made woman, but the effect was still statuesque rather than feminine. Above the waist she had on some sort of bunchy jersey, thick-knitted and full of unnecessary dimensions. It was in fact a good deal more revealing than the tight-stretched leggings beneath it, I think because the contours it covered were mobile. The almost silver hair was brushed back behind her head, and she seemed to have next to no make-up on. She was an astonishing figure to discuss your domestic arrangements with, but I still did not know at all what to make of her.

We came to the doorway at almost the same moment, but she did not check her stride at all. She marched straight in, and I stood aside in the narrow hallway to let her through. She said, "Now let's have a look at this cottage of yours." She turned not, as I had expected, right into the kitchen, but left into the sitting room I had just come from. She walked into the middle of it and stood there with her back to me, looking about her, while I watched her from the door. I was immediately less sure than I had been about the decency of those trousers. Also, apart from what there was to see of her, there was no question that she was more attractive when you could not see her face, or rather when she was not looking at you. Whatever it was, there was a quality in her that ran counter to the sheer female splendor of her body. I have never been one of those people who would really like to have their women unconscious, but I had a feeling that one or both of us would have to be quite a little drunk before I could make love to Mrs. Callender.

I had just reached this unedifying conclusion when she turned and said, "What do you want to drink, by the way? Whisky?" This was not a casual invitation, but a question of housekeeping. The shops were unbelievably remote, and in any case, once ashore, I had no transport. I was therefore to draw my rations from the house. I assumed I should be in some form charged for them, but there was no cash transaction involved. It was the army all over again, and in my present mood of willful irresponsibility it suited me very well.

I said, "Yes, please. That covers everything. I don't drink during the day, and in any case I'm not a beer man."

She nodded. "Remember to collect a bottle next time you're up at the house." She stood there facing me. I do not know which of us was in fact the taller, but we were pretty well eye to eye. I had the curious feeling that she was sizing me up physically. Men do this to other men instinctively, even in the most civilized settings, but I do not think I had ever had a woman do it to me before, not quite like this. Of course a woman will look a man over if she finds him attractive enough to warrant her consideration, but this was something different. I had an absolute conviction that the question in both our minds was whether I was physically up to her, and that without any automatic assumption what sort of a struggle it would be. The curious thing was that I found this reassuring rather than disconcerting. As I have said, I was already, after years of lost touch, conscious of my body again as the asset it had once been. This sudden challenge, unspoken and wholly unexpected, was something I welcomed. I looked into those great gray eyes, mentally telling her to come on.

For what must have been quite a while neither of us said anything. Then she suddenly gave me that quick twitch of a smile I had seen once before when we were coming over on the boat. I had at that moment no doubt at all that she knew exactly what I was thinking. She moved across to me and tapped me lightly on the shoulder. "Come on," she said, "show me your cottage." I smiled back at her and, still smiling, turned and went out into the hall and through into the kitchen. For a second I did not hear her move. Then she came after me.

We discussed pots and pans and crockery in an entirely direct and businesslike way. By this I mean not only that there was no obvious intrusion of physical tension; there was also none of the archness which most women seem unable to avoid when talking to a solitary man about his domestic arrangements. I have never understood why it should be funny for a man, otherwise sexually normal, to be interested and efficient in a kitchen or about household cleaning. It is in fact the necessary corollary of what the women have been aiming at for the last century or so. But this does not prevent most of them from pretending that it is something mysterious and, as I say, slightly comic. I suppose it is a part of the defensive duplicity of the little woman. As usual, the little woman wants it both ways. The fact that Mrs. Callender was physically very far from little may have helped.

At any rate, we talked about my cooking arrangements as simply as we should, unless I was mistaken, talk about boats. It was only when she left the kitchen and marched across into the bedroom that there was a change. This had nothing to do with the traditional farcical associations of bedrooms, but because physical comfort was directly involved, we were brought back to our bodies. You could not be in Mrs. Callender's presence without being aware of her body, but for much of the time there was this curious detachment about it. Now the heat was suddenly on. The bed was made and the whole room tidy, but she yanked the covers back and, leaning over it, thumped the mattress and springs and felt the weight of the blankets. I should not have put it past her to kick off her shoes and climb in and try the thing for herself. I don't know what would have happened if she had. As it was, the whole performance was perfectly housewifely, but it had me, standing there watching it, in a sudden rage of straight physical desire. It was impossible to tell whether she was aware of the change, let alone whether it was something she contrived deliberately.

She began to put the bed together again. It was impossible, even in the state I was in, to miss the strength and efficiency of it. The bed would be better made by the time she had finished with it than it had been when I left it, and I reckon myself a good bedmaker. She turned her head without straightening up and spoke to me through the swinging curtain of bright hair. She said, "It doesn't seem too bad. Did you sleep all right?"

I suppose it was because I was a bit off balance that I passed up several things I was going to say and said the last thing that came into my head. I said, "Oh, yes. What about the last chap?"

She finished making the bed before she straightened up and turned round to face me. I do not think it really took very long. The delay was probably exaggerated by the drop in temperature.

"Mackie?" she said. "Oh, I think he was quite comfortable here. He never complained, anyhow."

"When was this?"

"Oh—it's some time since he went. He went very suddenly, and we didn't find it easy to replace him. It's not everyone's job, is it? And we have to be pretty particular about having anybody in a place like this." She smiled at me suddenly. "Well, you can imagine," she said.

I could imagine all sorts of things, but did not say so. I was for some reason concerned with the vanished Mackie, who I thought had slept in this bed, but in the cottage just up the hill. I wondered if Mrs. Callender had come down in skin-tight trousers to inspect his domestic comforts, and if so, what he had made of it. And of course why he had left suddenly, or indeed at all. I could not see myself wanting to leave, at least until some of the outstanding possibilities had been more fully explored.

I let myself, quite deliberately, dwell on the outstanding possibilities directly in front of me. I made no attempt to pretend I was doing anything else. I brought my eyes back to hers and smiled back at her. "I suppose so," I said. "I don't know yet how particular you have to be."

"Very particular indeed," she said. She had stopped smiling now. There was nothing playful or kittenish in it at all. The tone was absolutely even. There was even something slightly menacing in it. I was no longer smiling either. We looked each other in the eye again, with complete gravity, as we had in the sitting room when she had first come in.

"I'll do my best," I said.

"Yes?" she said. "Let's see how it goes, then."

She went out into the hall and I followed. "I can let you have most of what you want from the house," she said. "What I can't I'll send for." It was an odd and miscellaneous list we had agreed on, and she had not made any sort of note, but I never doubted that the list would be implemented in detail. This was part of the formidable quality in her. There did not seem to be any real weaknesses.

"Oh, by the way," she said, "there's some stuff arriving at the landing stage at noon. Quite a lot. You may have to make two trips. But if you can be there by noon, you can make up your mind about that."

"I will," I said. She nodded and went out of the front door. I went out with her as far as the path and stood there, watching her walk uphill away from me in the brilliant sunlight. When she was about twenty yards away, the startling illusion of partial nakedness suddenly reasserted itself, and I watched her, breathless, until she disappeared over the hump of the path. She probably knew I was watching her, but she did not turn round or show her awareness of it in any way. As I have said, she was no doubt used to being watched.

I went down to the jetty and checked the fuel in the boat's tank. This had to watched, because there was no reserve at this point. Fuel had to be fetched as needed from the powerhouse on the far side of the island, and even there it was drawn only in a gallon can. There was plainly not going to be much in the way of pleasure cruising, but I did not see this as a restriction. I was too happy merely running the boat in the way of duty. Nor had I thought to ask what was coming or who was bringing it to the north shore. Whatever it was, it would be on the estate by that time and presumably accounted for to the Callenders' satisfaction. I was a part of the internal machinery, not a contact with the outside world. Feeling as I did about the outside world, I found this all to the good.

There was an hour to fill in before I need start, and I looked at my list to see what I could do to fill in the time profitably. Lacking Mrs. Callender's assurance, I had made careful notes during the morning's briefing. But now I relegated the terrace grass to a lower place on the list. I did not think I should see Mrs. Callender again that day.

CHAPTER 6

I CAME IN at the landing stage at between five and ten minutes to twelve and found no one about. I made fast to a ring halfway up the steps and walked up. The boat ran out a foot or two as I stepped off her and sat there motionless on the shining motionless water. It was an absolute calm and beginning to be very hot. The sky was a clear pale blue, but there was a haze gathering southward that I did not much like the look of.

I had been here three times already, but taken very little in. The evening before, I had got here in a daze and carried my collection of parcels down to the boat under the eye of a watchful and silent George while Mr. Callender put the car away. It seemed a very long time ago now. Early this morning I had been entirely preoccupied with Mrs. Callender and to a much less extent her suitcase. Later I had simply put Mr. Callender ashore and backed straight out. Now I had time to look about me.

It was very beautiful and profoundly peaceful, but there was not much to look at except the landscape. Just the solid stone garage with its steel door and heavily barred windows and the road, metaled but not tarred, stretching away eastward against the background of the big blue hills. Somewhere to the north I imagined there would be a boundary fence, but I could not see

it. The hills would belong to somebody else, but there was no mark of human occupation on them. Anywhere else I knew there would have been stone fences and a building or two, and almost certainly, on hills of this size, the visible scars of primordial human activity. Here there was nothing. The hills were as they had always been. Gray rocks stood up at intervals above the huge sweeping contours, but they were natural outcrops. It had not occurred to me that country of this sort still existed within a mere car journey, however long, of London.

Somewhere south and east of us, I did not know how far, the long skyline was broken by a prodigious steel spider's web, which I had seen against the last of the light as we came up the road. I had been almost beyond surprise by then, but I had roused myself to ask Mr. Callender what it was. "That?" he had said. "Oh, that's the Americans." In the half-light of that lost landscape it had seemed a sufficient explanation, and I had let it go at that. Now, with the sunlight hot on the huge emptiness, the thing seemed more prosaic and more incongruous. But whatever and wherever it was, it must be the only other man-made thing for miles apart from the Callenders' garage, and the mere recollection of it seemed to make the solitude more intense.

Because there was nothing else to hear, I heard the car engine long before I saw the car. I knew it was coming from eastward along the road, because that was the only place it could come from. But it was in fact simply a sound in the otherwise perfect silence. For all my ears told me, it might have been anywhere. The drone got louder, but still no car appeared. I could see quite clearly the point where the road dipped over a ridge and disappeared finally, but I found it impossible to judge how far this was from me. My eyes were quite unused to the long vistas and clear air, and I suspected that I was thinking everything nearer and smaller than it in fact was.

I waited, looking eastward along the road and filled with a quiet and entirely unreasonable apprehension. I suppose the approaching car represented in my mind the world I had retreated from. It was not so much that I was afraid of the world as that I did not want to be reminded of it. Southward across the flat water there was my new world, still hardly explored and full of promise, and I wanted to surrender to it with a mind emptied of earlier associations. In my present state of mild shock I could manage this, but the thing was precarious, and I resented anything that threatened it.

The car appeared suddenly over the crest of the road. It looked minute, and disappeared almost at once into a dip I had not known was there. I thought it was some sort of van, as indeed I might have expected, and it was dark-colored. Beyond that I could not tell much. It had obviously been much further away than I had allowed for. The noise of the engine, muffled in the dip, seemed as far away as ever. When the car reappeared it was almost startlingly close. It was a sizable van, a half-ton at least, and painted an all-over gray-black. It did not seem to have any lettering on it. I suppose I had been expecting some sort of delivery vehicle, or at least a carrier's van, but this was plainly private. If it was private, I could only assume it belonged to the Callenders. I need not have worried about the outside world. This was just another part of the machine. I was still well on the inside.

There was a single driver, a red-faced chap, peering at me intently as he brought his van to a halt on the turning circle in front of the garage. I came up to the side of the cab, and he slid his window back. We nodded to each other. Despite his jolly red face, he seemed a little wary. He said, "Hullo, there."

"Hullo," I said. "I'm Mackie's successor." I don't know why I said this, except perhaps that I had had the vanished Mackie on my mind since earlier that morning. He knew who I was anyway. There would not be anyone else waiting about in these parts.

"Oh, ay," he said. "I thought maybe you'd be following Mackie." I had the impression he found this in some way amusing, but he was a man with a naturally sardonic turn to him. I felt myself that what I had said was rather silly, but there was nothing now I could do about it. He said, "You'll have the boat there?"

I nodded, and he got out of his van, moving a little stiffly, as if he had driven some distance. He walked up the bank easing his shoulders and stretching his legs. At the top he stopped and surveyed the empty landing stage with the boat on its painter at the foot of the steps. He did this quite deliberately, as if he was really looking for something, only I could not think what he could be looking for. Then he nodded again and came back to the van. "We'd best get the stuff out," he said. "You'll be needing to make more than one load of it." He took some keys out of his pocket and unlocked the doors at the back of the van. It was not by any means full, but unless the stuff was a good deal lighter than it looked, it would obviously more than fill the boat to its safe capacity, even in these conditions.

I said, "Yes, I'm not taking all that in one go." I put rather a decisive edge into it. I did not like this big man being amused at me, and wanted to show I was captain of my own ship.

He gave me a quick look and nodded again. "That's right," he said. He got into the van and began shifting some of the cases round. "I'll hand it out to you," he said. "Some of it's heavy."

I came up to the doors and he lifted a case and put it into my arms. It was heavy enough, but I took it casually and stood there waiting. "I'll take something else with it," I said. He gave me another of his quick glances but did not say anything. He put another case on top of the first. The combined weight was just about up to my limit, but I said, "Right," and turned to go up the bank with it. I went to the bottom of the steps, put the cases down a few steps up and turned to pull the boat in. I was slightly out of breath, but no worse. I got the cases stowed. When I went up again, he had got more cases out of the van and even brought two or three to the top of the bank.

Any job of this sort compels a curious sort of intimacy between the two people engaged on it, but this can go two ways. Either a sympathy develops or the thing becomes antagonistic and competitive. Here there was no sympathy at all, but the antagonism was all of that oddly muted, sardonic kind which seemed natural to the man I was working with. So far as I was concerned, I was competing with myself as much as I was with him, and I was getting a good deal of satisfaction out of the way the competition was going. I went up and down the steps and on and off the boat, all in the hot sun, with the sweat running into my eyes and my clothes sticking to me, but with my muscles taking the strain equably and coming up for more. I think I got more satisfaction out of those twenty-odd minutes than I had out of years with the Platemakers. When the boat was well down in the water but nicely trimmed, I came up to the top of the bank and found him leaning against the side of the van with a few cases beside him. I said, "Is there much more?"

He was much more interested in me now, but as wary as ever and still slightly amused at something. He said, "There's two or three more cases in the van."

"I can't take any more aboard this trip," I said. "Get the rest out of the van and I'll come back for it." I turned without waiting for his reply and went down to the boat. When I was twenty yards out I looked back, but there was nothing to see. I made what speed I could and at the other end ran the boat hard up on to the sand. I stacked the cases well up from the water, working more slowly now when there was no one to see, but still keeping the job moving fairly systematically. When I headed out again for the north shore, I felt relaxed and very solitary. The bracing irritation of the red-faced man's presence had left me, and I was alone on the job, and not unhappy with it.

I made the boat fast and went up the steps, cheerful in the enormous silence. At the top of the bank I stopped dead. The van was still there, with the red-faced man leaning against it looking up at me, almost exactly as I had left him. But there were more cases on the ground now, and the van doors were shut.

"Still here?" I said.

"Ay," he said. "There's just this lot to come."

I nodded, hoping I had not pulled up with too much of a jerk when I saw him. "I'll take them," I said.

When I had the last of the cases on board, he came up to the top of the bank and watched me cast off. "I'll be getting along, then," he said.

I said, "You do that. I'll be seeing you, I expect."

"Maybe," he said. He raised a hand and vanished over the top of the bank. I was not very far from the landing stage when a thought occurred to me. I cut the engine completely. The way came off the loaded boat at once, and in the silence I heard the van making off eastward along the road. This time he really had gone. I re-started the engine, put the drifting boat on course and settled down for the return trip. I knew, of course, that the hardest part of the job lay ahead. Having got the stuff ashore, I had to take it piecemeal up to the house, and this was a much longer haul than from the garage to the foot of the steps. But, as far as I knew, I had the whole afternoon to do it in, and any job that entailed repeated visits to the house obviously offered a chance of seeing Mrs. Callender. Also, I was in that stage of conditioning when I welcomed any laborious job for its own sake. I was in love with my physical strength again, and this is as much a basic and inalienable satisfaction to a man as to be in love with her own looks is to a woman.

By now the whole sky to the south and east had lost its innocence. The haze had spread almost to the zenith, and low down there were dark shapes beginning to come up that looked very like thunderheads. Only westward the sky was still brilliant, and the water threw back the brilliance of the sky. Something, a mere speck in the shining distance, caught my eye. It was very difficult to focus it clearly, but I was fairly certain it was a boat. If so, it was the first I had seen, and I wondered where it had come from. It was a long way westward, and the obvious explanation did not then occur to me.

I got the second load of cases on shore, made the boat fast and began to consider the business of getting the stuff up to the house. It was all easy enough to handle. There were a lot of cardboard cartons, the usual things that tinned foods came in, and an even larger number of wooden cases, unmarked, nailed tight down and varying a good deal in weight. These might contain almost anything. More than ever I got the impression of a complete private consignment, packed specially for the purpose. I thought that probably the red-faced man, wherever his headquarters were, acted as a sort of receiving depot for the establishment. Unless I was mistaken, he had done a good deal of the packing himself before loading the stuff on his van. It all made sense, with the sort of transport problems involved. It was also very efficient and highly organized. And of course expensive. Whatever had made the Callenders choose to live on an island, they had made a very thorough job of it.

I had had nothing to eat since breakfast. It was now well on into the afternoon, and I found I was very hungry. Even this I welcomed. I had not, considering the life I had been leading, had very much soft weight on me, but it had been there, and in my new preoccupation with my body I wanted it all off. Nevertheless, I should not do myself any good running indefinitely on an empty stomach. I picked up the first case that made a reasonable load and walked with it up to the cottage. I put it down on the path, went inside and got myself something to eat and drink. I stiffened a bit, of course, as soon as I sat down, but it was too sultry to get cold, and the food went down like fuel to the furnace. I sat for perhaps a quarter of an hour. Then I went out, picked up the case and set off up the path to the house.

There did not seem to be anyone about. I went to the side door and knocked. I expected the taciturn George, but when the door opened, it was Fifi on the other side of it. She was dressed exactly as when I had first seen her and, compared with my sweat and sunburn, looked very elegant. Her clothes made no apparent concession to the heat, but the effect was as good as ever. She said, "Oh, is it the stuff come?"

"That's it," I said. "There's quite a lot of it."

"Yes, George said there would be. Will you put it in here?" She turned and led the way into a small room opening off to the right just inside the door. It was completely empty. Plastered walls, a bare board floor, a single window, nothing else. "If you'll put in all in here," she said, "George will sort it when he comes back."

I had already been long enough on the island to find this surprising. There was, virtually, nowhere to go. "Comes back from where?" I said.

She looked at me for a moment. If the look was suggestive, it was only because almost everything she did was suggestive. I still did not know how far the suggestion was well grounded, but she was that sort of person. She said, "He's out in the boat with Mrs. Callender. They're fishing."

I thought of the speck away to the westward. It had looked a very long way away. It must have been the rowing boat, presumably with the outboard motor fixed. I smiled at her as disarmingly as I knew how. "It's a bright day for fishing," I said. "But if they're spinning they may get something."

She tossed her head at that. "Mrs. Callender knows all about fishing," she said.

From what I had seen of Mrs. Callender in a boat I did not doubt this. I nodded. "I'll bring the stuff up," I said. "It will take some time, I'm afraid."

"Yes," she said. "Well, I'll leave the door open. Just bring it up and put it in here. Will that be all right?"

"That will be fine," I said. I smiled at her again, and this time she smiled back. Then I turned and went out of the door and down the path.

I do not know how many times I made the journey. I was under no compulsion now to take more than I could comfortably manage at a time. It was a long slow haul rather than an agonized effort, and I was still getting satisfaction out of it. Most of the time Fifi was not to be seen. Then when there were not more than half a dozen cases to come up, she suddenly appeared behind me in the doorway as I dumped my load.

She looked at the stacked cases and then at me. Her green eyes were wide open, as I had seen them the first time. "Oh, there's an awful lot," she said. "Aren't you tired?"

Even with Fifi I rejected the heroic gesture. "I am," I said. "I'm getting quite tired. But I don't mind, to be honest. I think it's doing me good."

She said, "Oh, I don't know. Don't make yourself too tired. Shall I get you some tea?" She was genuinely concerned. There was a nice person under all that compulsive provocativeness.

"Not yet," I said. "I've almost finished. And then I really must have a clean-up."

"All right, if you're sure." She thought for a moment. "Mrs. Callender said you were to take a bottle of whisky," she said.

I laughed outright. "You're dead right," I said. "I'll be wanting it presently. But not just yet."

She was never quite sure when I laughed, but I had no time

now to stop and explain that I was laughing because I found her so charming. "I'll get it for you," she said.

"Please do," I said. "And I'll get up the rest of these damned cases."

I did not see her again until my next-to-last trip. She had a bottle in her hand. "Here it is," she said.

I said, "Hold it, Carrie. There's just one more case to come up. You don't mind if I call you Carrie?"

She said, "I don't mind at all," and I turned and went down the path for the last case. When I came up with it as far as the cottage, she was there at the door with the bottle still in her hand.

"I've brought it down for you," she said.

I said, "Bless you, Carrie." I put the last case down on the path as I had the first one and went to the cottage. "Bring it in," I said.

I went in ahead of her and turned into the sitting room. She went into the kitchen, and I heard her put the bottle down on the table. The sun had gone in at last, and it was surprisingly dark in the cottage after the glare. I came out of the sitting room into the hall and at the same moment she came out of the kitchen. We collided gently. It was a purely involuntary collision, but she was a nice person to collide with. I did nothing to take myself away from the softness pressed against me, and just for a moment she hesitated to take it away from me. It was one of the most decisive hesitations in my life. I put my hands round her, and she stood there, looking up at me. I did not even kiss her. I felt with both hands for the back of her dress, slipped a hook and ran the zip all the way down. Then I moved my hands to her shoulders and pulled the black dress forward off them and down her arms. I thought of it as the start of an entrancing exploration. You would not expect any woman of that shape to get by with only a dress. I was quite unprepared for the cascade of womanhood that overflowed as the shiny stuff came down off her. I pushed her away from me and looked at her, with her black hair piled over her head and her black frock clinging to her just below her hips, and all heaven in between. She looked for all the world like a colored plate out of an old *La Vie Parisienne*.

There was a shimmer of lightning in the dusk and then a startlingly loud roll of thunder. I took no notice of it at all. For myself, I did not care if it snowed.

CHAPTER 7

IT WAS A FINE BRIGHT MORNING with a fresh breeze blowing from the west. But then it had been fine before sunset the evening before. I remembered—I did not think I should ever forget—the sight of Fifi, with my yellow oilskins flapping over her black frock, belting up the path ahead of me in the flickering dusk, with the rain coming straight down like a waterfall and the thunder grumbling almost continuously. I had gone up after her, carrying the last case, in my trousers and shirt, which could in any case do with a wash. She had flung the oilskins off at the door and dived into the house to refurbish herself. I had dumped the case and gone out, shutting the door behind me. I picked up the oilskins and started to walk down with them. Then, as a thought struck me, I stopped and put them on over my already drenched clothes.

I was glad I had, because just before I got to the cottages I saw George and Mrs. Callender coming up the path. They were fully weather-proofed and carried their fishing gear. Even so, Mrs. Callender looked superb. I wondered if there were any clothes that would not set her off. I supposed frills of any sort. She said, "Did you get the stuff up before it started?"

"Nearly all of it," I said. "I waited for the last few bits, but it looked like going on for a while, so I brought it up. It's all up now."

The thunder rolled again, and I thought that there was one very wet case and all the rest dry. I hoped George would be too busy to sort them out until next morning. She just said, "Good," and I stood aside to let them go up the path. And then, hardly a quarter of an hour later, the rain had stopped and a breeze had rolled up the cloud from the west, and there was a long brilliant evening ahead. The flickering dusk of an hour before seemed like another day.

But it was not. There was the whisky bottle, opened, on the kitchen table with two used glasses beside it and a certain amount of confusion in the bedroom. I had tidied up and given myself another whisky. Then straight physical exhaustion had hit me like a rubber truncheon. I had flung my clothes off and eaten something, standing naked in the kitchen, while the bath-water was running. I just about remembered falling into bed. But today I felt fine, and dwelt on the details of the previous evening with a placid, early-morning pleasure.

Even so, I wondered how much of a complication Fifi might be. I liked Fifi very much, but I never doubted that she was a complication, not the main issue. And I wondered, there by the kitchen window, with the sunlit water rolling across below me, what was happening in the house up the hill. It was not George I was worrying about, as I suppose it should have been. It was Mrs. Callender. I do not think, looking back, that there was ever a time when she did not dominate the entire course of events, or failed to make her domination felt. Even when I did not see her, she was always there.

There was a temptation to find work to do away from the house, and to let the repercussions of the previous evening, if there were any, find their way to me. But I was in two minds about this. At any rate, I went down to the boats, which were both on the beach by the jetty. The small boat usually lived on the other side of the island, by the powerhouse. There was no beach there, but they had made a slip for her, so that she could be pulled right up out of the water without much difficulty. The outboard was kept in the powerhouse. But last night they had run her on to the beach and come straight up the path. I wondered why they had done this and where they had been when Fifi ran up from the cottage to the house. On the beach, I thought, in which case they could not have seen her. And in the conditions they might well have decided to make straight for the nearest landing point and perhaps the simplest maneuver. All the same, I wondered.

The boats sat side by side on the beach, shining in the sunlight, but full of rainwater. The small boat still had the outboard on the transom, cocked up on its bracket with its canvas cover tied over the upper works. I did my own boat, working away at the hand pump and finishing off with the mop. She would soon dry in these conditions, and fresh water leaves no legacy of damp, as salt does. Then I took the outboard off the small boat and rolled her over on her side. She was solidly built and, with all that water in her, surprisingly heavy, but I got her up to the point where all but the odd pint or two slopped out over the gunwale on to the beach. I let her down, mopped her out and wondered about the engine. I still had half a mind to go up to the house, but a wet outboard needs to be run. Even if it was not my particular charge, I did not like leaving it there in the damp canvas bag. I put the engine back on the transom, made sure that the oars were in the boat and pushed off from the beach. We drifted outward and eastward while I was taking the cover off the engine and getting her ready to start. When she started, at the third or fourth pull, I found we were pointing almost due east. I started to turn inshore, hesitated and held on course. The boat lived at the powerhouse, and to the powerhouse she should go. In the meantime, I would circumnavigate at least the eastern half of the island, which I had otherwise no excuse for doing.

I held well out from the shore. Where there was beach and bank, the land went down sharply enough into deep water, but in places a line of rocks ran out, and here I did not feel too sure. If I had to hole a boat, it would be better not to hole one during an unauthorized run in a boat I had not been put in charge of. I motored slowly on round the green empty edge of the island, wondering what would in fact happen if both boats went out of commission simultaneously. It suddenly occurred to me that we had, so far as I knew, no other means of communication with the shore. I suppose a telephone cable was possible, but it would be expensive and I had seen no sign of one. The post, unless I was mistaken, would be collected by the red-faced man, who would repackage it and bring it to the landing stage for me to pick up. There must be a standing arrangement about this, but I had not yet been told of it. For all I knew, any one of the cases I had brought over yesterday might have held repacked mail. But I had gone to get the stuff when I was told, and at fairly short notice. Now I came to think of it, I had no standing orders of any sort. There I was, on the spot and available to do whatever was wanted when it was wanted. There was no possibility of my not being available, as I was more or less within hailing distance so long as I was on the island. It was living over the shop with a vengeance. Feeling as I did then, I did not find it worried me. But I could see what Mrs. Callender had meant when she had talked of the need to find the right person for the job. It was logical, once you had settled for that degree of isolation, but it was odd.

The eastern end of the island was higher than the rest. It was also greener, with quite a growth of trees. None of the buildings was visible from out where I was. The island might have been uninhabited. I edged slowly round, and suddenly opened up the small inlet that led to the powerhouse. I had not seen the powerhouse from the water before and had not realized what a considerable structure it was. There was a wall of dressed stones going straight down into deep water, so that a boat could get alongside in any reasonable conditions. At the top of the wall there was a paved causeway a yard or two wide, with the wall of the powerhouse itself and its double doors running up on the far side. The derrick was stepped in the stonework of the causeway, so that its arm swung out over the boat on one side and into the door of the powerhouse on the other. Like so much else, it was an efficient, laborious and expensive solution to what seemed to be an arbitrary difficulty. I had never met anyone like the Callenders for backing their fancy to the hilt.

The slip was at the head of the inlet, just under the powerhouse on its eastern side. From the top of the slip you turned left-handed to get to the causeway. The powerhouse had windows on this side, set high up in the wall, but the only door seemed to be the one on the south, by the derrick. I had no doubt that the whole thing had been designed and built by the same man as the garage on the north shore. Whoever he was, he did a solid job and made very few concessions to mere appearance. I went cautiously up the inlet with the engine four-stroking. When I cut the engine altogether, I heard the motor running in the powerhouse.

This was disconcerting. I had assumed that there would be no one here at this time of the morning. I had meant to put the boat up on the slip, leave the engine wherever it would go and walk back to the cottage. Although I had not said so to myself in so many words, I should probably have made a detour round the house. Then the job would have been done, and I could have reported it later as a matter of course. Now here I was, actually bringing the boat in, and there was someone, presumably

George, of all people, in the powerhouse above me. I could not ignore him. The outboard was kept in the powerhouse, and the obvious thing was to take it along to the door and hand it in to whoever was there. In fact there was nothing else I could possibly do. Only I wished now that I had left the boat on the beach until someone had told me what they wanted done with it.

I grounded the boat gently and carried the engine up to the top of the slip. Then I pulled the boat well up and made her fast. I did all this in a sort of charade of routine efficiency, just in case anyone was watching me from the powerhouse. At the same time, I did it as quietly as possible, just in case no one was. Out here the powerhouse motor made no more than a deep drone, but inside that solid stone building the noise would be quite considerable, and I didn't think anyone working there could have heard my cautious arrival. Whoever he was, I had to meet him sometime, but I wanted it to be in my own time, when I was ready to put the best possible face on it. I did not want to be challenged suddenly from behind or over my head. I did not think this was by any means all because of Fifi and the night before. Fifi was still no more than a complication. There was something about the very tight-knit Callender organization that made it very easy to feel an outsider. In this curious, compelled coexistence, feeling an outsider was an awkward business, and I wondered whether the Fifi affair was going to make it better or worse. When I had done everything with the boat that could possibly need doing, I picked up the outboard and walked back with it towards the door of the powerhouse.

The door was shut. The noise of the engine was louder here, and I caught the characteristic whiff of diesel exhaust. I put the outboard down against the wall and wondered what I ought to do. With its high barred windows and shut door, the powerhouse looked extraordinarily secretive. There is in any case something a bit disturbing about walking into a place looking for someone who is not expecting you, and here the feeling was especially strong. I had not seen very much of George Benson, but in his way he was as secretive as the powerhouse. Between them they took some intruding on.

But the thing was not logical, and in any case now I had come so far there was nothing else to do. I tried the door and it opened under my hand. The sound of the plant rose to a steady drumming and the smell of oil flowed out to meet me. There was plenty of light from the windows, but the place seemed shadowy and colorless after the brilliance outside. I knew very little about such things, but it all seemed to me impressively big and powerful. Only George Benson was not there.

The far wall had control panels of dials and switches, but in the middle of them there was what looked like a small steel door. I didn't know what it could lead to. I tried to compare the space I could see with the outside length of the building, but it was difficult to judge with all that plant in it. I thought there might be another room on the far side of the steel door, but I could not be certain. If there was, it would not be very big.

I moved towards the door, and a voice, very sharp and penetrating above the noise of the engine, said, "Stand still where you are." I stood still and then, when nothing happened, turned round to see where the voice had come from. I would not say I expected to find a man pointing a gun at me. That was a thing which had never happened to me, and I should have been uncomfortably surprised if it had. But it did occur to me, as I turned, that the words sounded very much as if somebody was.

In fact no one was. George was standing just inside the door of the powerhouse. He was looking at me with all the concentration in the world, but he had nothing in his hand except a hammer. It was, as I found later, an effective weapon at short range, but he could hardly have knocked me over with it at the full length of the powerhouse and with all that machinery between us. He must have yelled the first time, because when he spoke again, probably in his normal voice, I could not hear what he said.

I looked at him. He did not move. He just stood there, with the door half open behind him, looking at me. "I've brought the boat round," I said. I think probably he couldn't hear what I said either. At any rate, he took no notice.

"Come back here," he said. I could see the effort he put into it, and this time the words came to me perfectly clearly. I walked back towards him. When I got close to him, he motioned me out through the door. I went outside and he followed me. There was not much expression on his face. He looked extremely watchful, but then I had never seen him look anything else. I don't think he shut the door behind him, but out here the noise of the engine was much less obstructive, and we could make each other hear in normal voices.

He said, "Never go near that end of the floor. It can be very dangerous." He let this sink in, watching me to see if I took it seriously. I thought he might have explained the danger, but I did not doubt he meant what he said. I said nothing. "The powerhouse isn't your job in any case," he said. "Why have you come?"

I said again, "I've brought the boat round. Where shall I put the motor?"

"Did Mrs. Callender tell you?"

"Mrs. Callender?" I said. I think I overdid it a bit. It must have sounded almost as if I had never heard of her. "No, no one told me. The boat was on the beach, but I knew it was kept here, so I brought it round."

He said, "The boats don't go out without orders." He said it quite tonelessly. I think the form of words was meant to suggest that we were all in this together, but I was left in no doubt that, even if he was not actually giving me orders, he was putting me straight.

Quite deliberately, I played the fellow servant. I did not feel like this about him at all, but it seemed the proper approach. I raised my eyebrows and smirked at him knowingly. I said, "Pretty strict, aren't they?"

I should hesitate to say that I had ever seen George Benson actually indicate any sort of emotion, but I thought something like a whiff of distaste showed for a moment at the corners of his mouth. At any rate, he refused to join the conspiracy.

"The boats are essential if the place is to work," he said. "Mrs. Callender has to know where they are." Once more, though in a different form of words, I was up against the now familiar proposition. You had to have boats. As usual, I agreed.

"Of course," I said. "I can see that. But I didn't take her out. I mean, not away from the island. I simply brought her round from one side to the other. Still—"

He cut across this. It did not seem like a piece of deliberate rudeness. It was more as though he had been following some other train of thought and had simply not heard me speak. He said, "Where have you put the outboard?"

I turned and pointed to it, leaning against the wall behind me. I had no intention of picking it up and taking it any further. He nodded and went across to it, looking it over as if he expected to find something wrong with it. Of all incongruous things, he reminded me of a cow whose calf has been in strange hands. There was the same mixture of suspicion and anxiety. I thought of several things to say, but said none of them.

I said, "I'll be getting back, then." He nodded, but again I was not sure whether he had really heard me. I walked back along the causeway. The boat sat there innocently at the top of the slip. I was more than ever thankful I had kept her off the rocks. I wondered if George would go and look her over when he had finished looking over the engine, but didn't wait to see.

I should have liked to have another look at the northern end of the powerhouse, but I didn't wait for this either. When I got to the top of the rise, I looked at the hills of the north shore, standing up huge and perfectly empty across the reach of blue, ruffled water. Just for a moment I saw them, for the first time, not only as something I had escaped from, but also as something out of reach. No doubt I should go to the north shore often enough. But the land when I got there was still Callender land, and someone, Mr. Callender or the red-faced man or someone I had not yet met, would be waiting for me. I did not think I minded about this, but I wondered.

CHAPTER 8

I SAW NO ONE from the house all that day. The breeze died out, and the day was as hot as the one before. I worked all day in the open, wearing only a pair of shorts. The sun had touched up my skin through my shirt the day before, and now it got properly to work on me. It was a surprisingly strong radiant heat, but I did not usually burn sore, and the idea of a tan suited my present mood. I enjoyed myself very much.

When I felt I had done enough, I made myself a pot of tea. Then I collected a clean shirt and a pair of trousers and went out to have a swim. The sun was well over into the west, and I made for the western end of the island. There was a track running that way. It wound between the rocks and was well sunk into the soft top of the island. I thought the stones had come this way from the quarry when they built the house and cottages, but now it was only a green channel through the bracken and heather. I went past the mouth of the quarry to the lip of the land, but found awkward-looking boulders standing among the motionless sunlit water instead of the sandy beach I wanted. I turned right-handed under a green hummock topped with rock, and when I came back to the water, I found sand. I went down through a cleft in the bank and saw Mrs. Callender not fifteen yards from me. She was standing with her hands on her hips, staring out to the west, where the distant hills closed in gradually on the long vista of water.

I hesitated and then walked on. Then she moved one of her hands and I stopped dead. The hand went almost absent-mindedly to the top of her cotton skirt and fiddled there. Without taking her eyes off the long stretch of bright water in front, she undid the waist of the skirt and slipped it down off her. Sooner or later she would turn, and I moved back until I could only just see over the top of the bank. I could not have taken my eyes off her if I had heard a galloping horse behind me, but I heard nothing and no one came. I stood there watching her in a frenzy of apprehensive fascination. She took off all her clothes, still with the same piecemeal absent-mindedness that was more disturbing than the most highly calculated strip-tease. Then she put her hands back on her hips and stood there, exactly as I had first seen her, but naked, still staring out into the west and busy with whatever it was she was thinking about. At last she roused herself with a jerk of her shoulders, stooped and reached for the bundle on the sand beside her. The vision was over. I stepped back out of sight and then went back up through the cleft, breathless with a sort of regretful ecstasy. I was full of mere male desire, of course, but what I had seen had also been very beautiful. I waited until I thought she must be into her swimming things. Then I turned and went down through the cleft and straight out on to the beach. Her clothes were there on the sand with a towel over them, and she was fifteen yards out from the beach, swimming steadily westward with an easy powerful crawl.

My dilemma was now one of social procedures. I still wanted my swim, I should like to swim with Mrs. Callender, I thought I swam as well as she did, though certainly no better. The water was presumably free for all. The fact remained that to appear suddenly swimming alongside her would be an intrusion, and I thought any intrusion might be unwelcome. Even on my present judgment of her, I fancied that she would resent my having intruded on her mental preoccupation a good deal more than my having watched her undress. But I did not want her to know I had done either.

I was still wondering what to do when she stopped swimming and rolled over on her back. She must have been nearly thirty yards out from the beach. Like everyone else in the world who has ever swum out from a beach, she put her head up and looked back. I do not know why you do it. To see how far you have swum, to see if your clothes are all right, perhaps just to make sure the beach is still there. She saw the beach as and where she had left it, with me standing on it, looking out after her and wondering what to do next. She answered my question without any apparent hesitation at all. One long golden arm came up out of the water and beckoned me in.

I raised a hand in acknowledgment and got into my swimming trunks in the shortest possible time. As far as I know, she was still watching me, but I did not waste time being coy about it. Nor, on the other hand, did I brandish my nakedness at her, even at thirty yards range. I simply did what I should have done if I had been alone on the beach, because that seemed the natural thing to do. I ran a few steps down to the water and began to wade out. The shock almost knocked the breath out of me. The sun was still hot on my chest and shoulders, but the water was deadly cold. I went on without hesitation, but now I was play-acting every inch of the way. Left to myself, I should have let my lower half accustom itself to the chill of the water before I put my top half in, but now I was drawn on by that beckoning arm. I caught my breath and stumbled on. When the water was just above my waist, I plunged forward and started to swim. The effort beat off the cold to some extent, but I still found it almost frightening. And the water was dead and clinging. It had none of the ebullience of sea water and did nothing to help you. It simply lay there in an inert, chilling mass, leaving you to make your way through it as best you could. I kept on swimming, because Mrs. Callender was out there ahead of me, but I did not like it at all.

She trod water, watching me swim. Then, when I was ten yards or so from her, she rolled over and started to swim out again. She swam an easy stroke, as if she was waiting for me to draw up alongside her, but the pace was deceptive, and it didn't take me long to see that although I was swimming fairly hard, I was gaining on her only very slowly. As I have said, my muscles were getting into better condition, but for this sort of swimming in water like this I had no wind at all. I was still just gaining on her, but I was starting to lose form, and my chest felt terrible. If this was some sort of test, I was going to fail it. All the time we were getting further out from the beach.

If it is not a matter of survival, the moment always comes when the body refuses to play up any longer to the vanity or ambition of the mind. Suddenly I just stopped swimming and rolled over on to my back with my legs doubled up and my chest going in and out like a concertina. Mrs. Callender must have called the thing off a fraction of a second earlier, because I found myself right up against her. She wore no sort of bathing cap, and her hair floated all round her head in the cold motionless water. She smiled at me, a strange mermaid's smile. I could only shake my head at her and gasp. If I smiled back, it was little more than the rictus of a man at the limit of his powers. "Too cold for me," I said.

She stopped smiling. I do not think she showed any concern, not then, but she spoke perfectly seriously. "It is cold," she said. "And you're not used to it. Let's go back. But take your time."

I turned in the water and saw the beach a good deal further away than I had expected. I didn't really doubt my ability to get there, but it was not to be taken wholly for granted. I took a few deep breaths and then dropped my face into the water and started swimming again. I swam slowly, streamlining every movement in a desperate conservation of energy. Beside me, Mrs. Callender swam stroke for stroke.

Even now, when I had done with bravado, I was on my mettle. Left to myself, I should have stopped at least once during that swim back to the beach, to get my breath and gather my wits, however much I wanted to be out of that unnaturally cold water and on to the sunlit sand. As it was, I kept on swimming, still stroke for stroke with the beautiful relentless arms that cut the water beside me with the rolling head of drowned silver hair between them. I was near my limit again when my leading hand touched bottom and the beach came up sharply under us.

We came out on to the sand together. I had no more pretense left in me. I dropped on to my knees with my head down, fighting to get my breath back. I could feel the sun on my back, but it didn't penetrate my cold-sodden body. Then a pair of arms came round my shoulders and Mrs. Callender pulled me to her. She said again, "It's too cold for you. You're not used to it. You shouldn't—"

She broke off and simply held me, and I knelt there with my face against her thinly covered breasts. The skin was wet and cold, but there was warmth under it. I was utterly unmanned with cold and exhaustion, and wanted only comfort. It was an unlikely, isolated moment, paradoxical to the whole relation between us. When I got my breath back, she took her arms from my shoulders and pushed me away from her. She said, "Now get yourself dry and get some clothes on. You'll warm up when you get moving." She was perfectly friendly and matter-of-fact about it, but the softness had gone out of her voice and the concern was no longer there. I lifted my head and looked at her. I was still very close to her. I smiled at her, more as I had smiled the day before. "Thank you," I said.

She hesitated, but found nothing to say. Instead, she gave me a quick smile and that same small shake of the head. Then she moved back from me and got up. We dried and dressed ourselves there on the beach in the soft, breathless sunlight. I was not really exhausted, simply winded and chilled, but my hands were clumsy and my balance uncertain. Mrs. Callender got herself dressed a few yards away from me with complete unconcern and perfect decency. We neither of us said a word. By the time I was dressed I was more myself again. The shock of that deadly water had worn off, and I felt stimulated and refreshed. But Mrs. Callender, cool, dressed, with her hair gathered neatly behind her head, was back behind the unimaginable depth of her defenses, and what had happened hardly ten minutes before was already as remote and unlikely as a dream.

We walked back slowly along the green track, dangling our damp swimming gear in our hands. It was like all the walks back from the sea I ever remembered, only it was not the sea behind us. I missed the feel and taste of salt on my skin and the smell of it in the air. This water was hostile. It lay deep and cold all round us, shutting us in. I had never thought of the sea like that. The sun was low now, and the elation of the day drained out of me as the warmth left the air. We had still not said anything. The track came out on to the north-facing slope halfway between the cottages and the house. When we got there I simply stopped. Mrs. Callender turned up the hill. Then she too stopped and turned, facing me down the slope of the path. She said, "Will you be all right?"

She was still, as she stood there, almost certainly the most magnificent woman I had ever seen. I had not felt this mixture of regret and desire since I was almost a child. There was something curiously adolescent about it. I said, "Mentally or physically?"

She considered this gravely. "I meant physically," she said.

"Physically I am fine," I said. "That water is hellishly cold and I am still not properly in condition. But I'm all right now. Mentally, I'm not so sure."

She put her hands, with her bathing things in them, behind her back and stood square in the path, with her feet slightly straddled. It was a rather masculine attitude, but nothing could ever make Mrs. Callender look masculine. She said, "How long had you been there?"

"Long enough," I said.

"I'm sorry. I didn't know you were there. I was a bit preoccupied, I'm afraid."

I said, "In God's name, why be sorry? It ought to be me."

"I'm sorry if I have contributed to your mental distress."

"Not distress," I said. "Unsettlement, if you like. There was a man who ran mad in the woods, wasn't there, for seeing what he was not supposed to see? It's one of those stories that stick in your head at school, because it is so very much a boy's experience."

She gave me a long hard look. "There was a man who was struck blind," she said. "Or so I seem to remember." Then she gave me her quick flash of a smile. "I must confess I could never see why. It seems very unreasonable. I have no wish for you to be struck blind."

"Or to run mad?"

She seemed to consider this. She still stood there with her hands behind her back and her head slightly on one side, looking at me down the slope of the path. She was completely grave again. Then she said, "I don't think I should mind a touch of madness."

"I don't think these things are easily managed," I said. "They merely happen, don't they?"

She said, "Not to me." She took her hands from behind her and brought her feet together. She was immediately and completely feminine, and all set to go up the path away from me. She said, "My husband will be at the landing stage at eleven tomorrow. Will you meet him?"

"I will," I said. Then I suddenly remembered George at the powerhouse and said, "If I may have the boat."

I could not for the life of me see whether she knew what I had in mind. She said, "I should prefer you to have the boat. I do not think you could swim the distance. I am quite sure he could not." She nodded slightly, turned and went off up the path. I went down. The hills of the north shore had the last of the sunlight laid all along them, throwing up their clefts and recesses with huge violet shadows. If the garage had been built on top of the bank, I could have seen it, but nothing broke the dark line of the shore. In this light the landing stage was quite invisible.

I turned over in my mind the question I had almost asked Mrs. Callender. I think I should have asked it if the thought of George had not put it out of my head. When she had said that her husband would be there at eleven next morning, what I had at once had in mind to ask was "How do you know?" If I had had a few more drinks at the Turk's Head that night instead of meeting Mr. Callender, I should have telephoned Ashwood from the call-box and said I should be back on the eight-seventeen. But Mr. Callender could not, as far as I knew, telephone his wife from anywhere. The answer, of course, was perfectly simple. She would have said, "That was the arrangement," and so it would have been. It would not have been in my place to say, "Why didn't he tell me?" All the same, I wondered why he had not. If his movements were plotted like this in advance, he could always say, "I'll be back at eleven on Thursday." On the other hand again, there was no reason why he should. There I was, on the spot and available at any time. That was part of the job.

77

I did not turn into the cottage at once. Instead I walked down to the jetty and checked the fuel tank of the boat. There was not enough in it to get me to the north shore, let alone to bring me and Mr. Callender back. I should have to draw some from George. But not tonight. He would not be at the power-house again tonight. For tonight the boat would lie there with an almost empty tank. And there was not enough wind to sail a matchbox.

I turned my back a second time on the level ice-cold water and went up the path. It was whisky I wanted, two whiskies and then some supper. The only other thing I wanted I was still in two minds about. I did not give Fifi a thought.

CHAPTER 9

THE BOAT CHUGGED on through the gray water. A fine rain fell endlessly, stippling the flat surface and making a soft continuous background to the throb of the engine. There was not a breath of air moving. Only the way on the boat brought the rain on to the front of my oilskins, so that they dripped steadily on to the floorboards between my rubber boots. Fisherman's weather, with the air as mild as milk.

Mr. Callender said, "Still fairly content?"

"More than content," I said. And less, I thought. Content, for the moment, to be discontented. But I could not explain the complication of my feelings, to him of all people.

He said, "Find plenty to interest you?"

I took my eyes off the water ahead for a moment and looked at him. He had the same friendly, slightly surprised smile that seemed to be his most characteristic expression. There was always this sense of underlying amusement, which I did not share but did not in any way resent. I had my own secret amusement now, and I smiled back at him. I nodded and looked ahead again. "Plenty," I said.

He did not say anything for a bit, but I knew he was watching me, and I put on my helmsman's face. There was nothing to look at except the gray outline of the island coming up ahead, but I concentrated on it as if we were rounding Portland Bill under sail in a southwesterly. He was not at home in boats as his wife was, and might let it pass. We were getting close in to the jetty when he spoke again.

"Well," he said, "you won't be leaving us yet awhile at any rate." Like quite a lot of the things he said, it was difficult to tell whether this was a statement or a question. It had something to do with the inflection of his speech. I still do not know whether it was deliberate.

I said, "Oh, I don't think so." For a second or so I hesitated. Then I said, "It wouldn't be easy to do in any case." I still kept my eyes ahead. I cut down the throttle to slow. You could hear the rain on the water more clearly now.

"Meaning?" he said.

I looked at him. It was only a quick glance, because now I really did have to keep my eyes on the boat. He was looking at me steadily. I thought there was slightly less amusement in it. "Well," I said, "it isn't an easy place to get away from, is it?"

"Ah, that?" he said. "You've only to ask." I cut the engine altogether, and the boat came silently in to the beach. The ripple died away on the pebbles, and now there was nothing to hear at all except the rain on the water. "All the same," he said, "I don't quite know where you'd go. You've rather burned your boats, haven't you?"

I stepped out and dragged the boat a little up the beach while he still sat in the stern. Then I held her, waiting for him to come ashore. We faced each other, with the boat's length between us and the rain dripping off the brims of our hats.

"I'm not breaking my heart over that," I said. "I'm not going back over that particular river in any case."

He got up and came down the boat. He had nothing with him but a briefcase, and he carried that himself. He nodded as he came. "Well, whatever river it is," he said, "let me know. But not yet, I hope."

When he was ashore I said, "Certainly not yet," and he nodded again and went on up the path.

The day went on very much as it had begun. It was not easy weather to do outside work in. I suppose I was still enough of an indoor worker to resent the choice between getting slowly wet through in ordinary clothes and getting into a sweat inside waterproofs. But nobody came down to see if I was working or not, and I had the feeling that nobody minded very much so long as I was there. With Mr. Callender at home the sense of preoccupation was very strong, though I cannot say that I had the slightest evidence to support it. When Mrs. Callender was alone in the house, I was aware of her presence the whole time, and I certainly allowed myself, not very explicitly, to believe that she was aware of mine. When the two of them were there, I was consciously alone. There was no resentment in this. I did not at any stage feel anything that could fairly be called jealousy of Mr. Callender. But he was a barrier, as he had been from the first moment I set eyes on his wife. The possibility that they were both consciously concerned with me did not occur to me. Rightly or wrongly, Fifi did not affect the thing either way.

In the evening a very slight breeze came in from the east and the rain stopped falling. The cloudbank never shifted and the air was as wet as ever. It was still very warm, but it got dark early. It was the sort of evening to breed restlessness, and I had not done enough during the day to make me ready to put my feet up. When I had washed up the supper things, I went into the sitting room. I turned on the reading lamp and drew the curtains, as I always did. Then I went out into the hall, shutting the door behind me. It was very dark, but there was the faintest gleam from a glass panel over the top of the front door. I let my eyes get fully used to the darkness. Then I opened the front door and went out. I shut it quietly behind me. I realized after I had done it that I had made as little noise as possible. Once this furtiveness was conscious, my turn uphill was inevitable. It was very dark and absolutely still. The wind had gone altogether. I had no reason to suppose there was anyone about. But there was the lit and curtained window of my sitting room, and there, for all you could tell from out here, was I in my chair, reading and smoking. But in fact I was out here, alone in the darkness. This gave me a disembodied feeling, as if I was halfway to being invisible. It was a game I used to play regularly on summer nights in my childhood, when they thought I was in bed. I think my sudden return to it was part of the mental swing back produced by this cataclysmic break in my life. I can only say that there was an extraordinary exhilaration in it. I seemed for the moment absolutely free, even from myself. I went on up the path, going as quietly as possible, until I saw the lights of the house up the hill. There was one bright light and I thought some faint, heavily masked lights from the front and a bright glow of reflected light from the western side, where the side door was. That would be the kitchen window.

The fact that my employers would not take kindly to my dodging round the house in the dark was too obvious for my mind to miss altogether, but I dismissed it with the assumption, not too closely examined, that I could always explain my presence if I had to. In the meantime that was all part of the excitement. It is no good playing hide-and-seek if no one is looking for you. I turned right-handed off the path on to the rougher going, making for a point well clear of the western side of the house. When I got there I turned again and came in very cautiously towards the light in the kitchen window.

There was a single bulb burning in the kitchen. The window was uncurtained, and I could see someone moving to and fro in the window. I was below the floor level of the house here, and could not see who it was or what they were doing. When I came to the low wall of the terrace, I moved along under it southward, until I was out of the direct rays of the light that shone out of the window. Then I scrambled up on to the terrace and stood there, taking things in.

It was Fifi, busy at the sink just inside the window. I suppose she was doing the after-dinner washing up. I could see enough of the room behind her to be certain there was no one else in it. There was only one other window at this end of the house. That was on the upper floor, above the kitchen window. It was probably one of the bedrooms. The window was quite dark, and I did not think there would by anyone up there at this time. My only preoccupation was with the side door, which I knew opened on to a passage, not direct into the kitchen. It was always possible that someone might come out of the door without showing themselves first in the kitchen, and once I was on the terrace there was no cover at all. My only chance would be to get back and under the terrace wall before whoever it was had got their eyes accustomed to the darkness.

I went back northward again, walking on the very edge of the terrace, where I could jump down into darkness if I had to. I walked until I was again out of the direct line of the kitchen light. Then I turned and went in towards the northwest corner of the house. If anyone came out of the side door now, I could get back round the corner of the house before they saw me. I came in very quietly along the wall of the house until I was close to the window. Then I moved out a little from the wall and looked in.

Fifi was still at the sink, working away steadily at the dishes. She was brightly lit, even with the bulb behind her, by the light reflected from the white walls of the kitchen. She had on some sort of light blouse, loosely buttoned down the front, and as she leaned over the sink I could see the deep cleft between her breasts as they swayed with her movements. Her hair was done lower on her head than I had seen it before, with most of it gathered over the back of her neck. She worked intently, and every now and then smiled slightly to herself. She made an extraordinarily attractive picture, and I would have given the world to know what she was smiling at. I even thought of tapping at the window, but had no idea what she would do if I did. She was still very much a stranger to me, despite what had happened two evenings before.

I wondered where George was. I did not know what his indoor duties were, but I should have expected him to be in the kitchen. I think it was him if anybody I expected to come out of the side door. With Fifi there in front of me, so unconsciously desirable in the bright window, he was the enemy I had to reckon with.

I watched Fifi for several minutes. She was an entrancing person, but I was no wiser at the end of it than I had been at the beginning. I left her still busy, and tiptoed back to the northwest corner and along the front of the house. The bright light I had seen came from a fanlight over the front door. Beyond it there was a big window, heavily curtained, with lights behind the curtains. I imagined this would be the sitting room, with the Callenders sitting in it. The curtains were tight-drawn, and despite the closeness of the night the window was shut top and bottom. Whoever was in the room and whatever was happening there, I could see and hear nothing.

I turned back towards the kitchen window, and then changed my mind and went eastward to the far corner of the house. I turned the corner and stopped dead. There was another window here, also lit and curtained. There was not the space for another room, and this must be an east-facing window of the same sitting room. I moved very quietly across it and then stopped again. The curtains were drawn well together in the middle, but at the far side the right-hand curtain had been pulled too far across, and there was a small gap between its outer edge and the side of the window. It left visible one narrow strip of the room. Even if I moved from one side to the other, the strip was not more than a few feet wide at its widest on the far side of the room, but both the Callenders were just visible in it. So, at least in part, was the door of the room.

All I could see of Mrs. Callender was the shining top of her head. She was sitting in a winged armchair facing three-quarters away from me. If she leaned forward I should be able to see her very nearly in profile, but at the moment her head was back, and I could see nothing but the gleam of silver-gilt hair over the chair back. Mr. Callender sat in a similiar chair, but almost facing me. His elbows rested on the arms of his chair and his hands were folded under his chin. He looked as if he was listening intently, but here again the window was shut, and I could not hear what he was listening to. From the way he was looking, I did not think it could be Mrs. Callender. It was more likely someone or something outside my line of vision on Mrs. Callender's right. His expression was serious but emotionally quite neutral. Then Mrs. Callender moved, and I saw his eyes turn slightly in her direction. She leaned forward so that I could just see the side of her head, though her face was still mostly turned away from me. She was speaking. She seemed to be speaking emphatically, and once one of her hands came up and made a gesture. When I saw her speaking like that, without being able to hear what she was saying, I felt once again the absolute conviction that she was not English. She may or may not have been talking English, but if she was, it was not native to her. When she had finished, her head went back again, and then Mr. Callender started to speak. He had hardly changed his position and still did not, talking over the top of his folded hands with his face slightly raised. I thought he was talking to his wife, but I could not be quite sure. He certainly looked at her occasionally while he spoke, but he moved little more than his eyes. I had one glimpse of his familiar, turned-in smile, but I saw it only once, and it was very fleeting. Then they were both, as far as I could tell, silent again, though whether they were listening or merely thinking I did not know.

I decided that there was better value to be had at the other side of the house. The air was still mild, but it was enormously damp, and my shoulders twitched with a slight shiver as I turned away from the window. I would have one more look at Fifi and then go down the hill and get to bed. The unreasonable elation was beginning to die out of me and what I was doing did not seem very sensible.

I tiptoed back along the front of the house, past the front window of the sitting room, past the front door, past the dark windows of what was probably the dining room, to the north-west corner of the house. When I got there I found that the kitchen light was out. Wherever Fifi was, she was no longer on show. I went to the kitchen window, but there was nothing to see. I hesitated, and was turning to go back down the hill when the side door opened, not a couple of yards from me, and some-one came out.

There was nothing I could do but face the door and pretend, if asked, that I was coming to the door for something. I had not yet thought what, but it was not particularly late and the thing was not wholly unreasonable. But of course all I did was to stand there frozen. My mouth was probably slightly open. There was a rustle of mackintosh, and a small dark figure shut the door gently behind it and walked quietly across the grass to the edge of the terrace. I knew at once that it was Fifi, and that she had not seen me.

I could have got back along the wall and round the front of the house, and she would never have known I was there. But the sight of her in the bright window only those few minutes before was too much for me. I wanted very much to touch her and speak to her. She was standing on the edge of the terrace looking out westward. Her hands were in the pockets of her mackintosh. I think she was letting her eyes get used to the darkness. I went a little way across the grass. I went very quietly, but she must have heard something. She began to turn around, and as she turned I whispered, "Carrie! Carrie, it's me. What are you doing out here?"

She spun round and her hands came out of her pockets. She said, "Ooh—" but it was little more than a gasp, barely vocalized. I went up to her and took hold of her hands. They were very warm, and she let me keep them. We stood there on the edge of the terrace, peering into each other's faces in the breathless murk. She said, "What are you doing here?" but it was whispered, and I had got in the same question first. I knew where I was with her. I said, "I came to see if I could see you."

She said, "Oh, you mustn't." She let go of one of my hands and led me by the other. She led me quickly round the southwest corner of the house, out of sight of the side door and beyond the range of the kitchen light, in case anyone turned it on. There was a bunch of outbuildings here which I had not yet seen the inside of. She said, "I don't know—" and stopped. I stood there, still holding her by the hand. Then she gave my hand a little shake in the darkness and said, "In here." She let go of my hand and opened the door of a shed close to the corner of the house. She went in and I went in after her. I shut the door behind me. It was completely dark in here, and the darkness smelled faintly of tar-oil and sacking. I groped for her and found she was leaning back against something soft, probably filled sacks. I unbuttoned her mackintosh and put my body against hers. Her clothes were thin, and I could feel the warmth of her through them. She could be in no doubt what I wanted.

She said, "It's all wrong. But I like you. I like you."

There are times when a woman will fasten on to some chance phrase and repeat it ecstatically, in a sort of rhythmical incantation. The phrase has to be a short one. I have heard some odd, inappropriate words used, but the woman is in any case speaking only to herself, and it does not matter much what she says. Fifi said, "I like you, I like you," until she stopped speaking altogether, and we simply clung to each other, panting a little in the tarry darkness.

Finally she said again, "I don't know—" I think she really did not. I didn't know anything much myself. I doubt if any two people ever acted more blindly or more completely to their mutual satisfaction and ultimate undoing. That was very nearly all we said to each other. It seemed very light when we went out of the shed, and the air smelled fresh and watery. The kitchen was still in darkness. We just whispered "Good night" to each other and she popped in at the side door of the house. I still did not know why she had come out or why I had either. The important thing was that we both had.

I went round to the front of the house. There were still lights behind the sitting-room curtains. I went on to the east-facing window and looked in through the gap. Mr. and Mrs. Callender were both leaning forward in their chairs, both looking towards the invisible corner on my right. Their faces were intent and quite expressionless. Then, almost at once, they both got up. A man walked obliquely across my line of vision. He passed behind the Callenders and went to the door. I saw only his back, but it was George, of course. There was no one else it could be.

Once George was on the move it was time I was gone. I did not risk going back along the front of the house. I went straight over the terrace wall at its nearest point, and set off in a long left-handed curve to pick up the path well below the house. I moved cautiously at first and then, as I got further from the house, as fast as I could safely go over the rough slope.

I was tired now. The glow which Fifi had left in me had died out, and a tremendous unease welled slowly up out of the back of my mind. I couldn't give it any very coherent form, but Fifi's "I don't know" stayed with me. The only thing I fastened on was the fact that during all that time in the sitting room George had been sitting down and that when he went the Callenders had both got up. This seemed odd, even in these egalitarian days. I knew very few people who kept manservants, even around Ashwood, but I thought the sort of people who did would scarcely be found sitting around chatting to them after dinner. Now that I came to think of it, George did not feel like a servant, for all his careful speaking. He felt formidable, more formidable than Mr. Callender. Whatever he was, I thought that my sense of unease was centered on him, and I did not like it.

I got on to the path and almost ran the rest of the way down to the cottage. The curtained glow in my sitting room shocked me as I came down to it. The suggestion of someone sitting inside waiting for me was almost unbearably strong. But it was only myself I had left there, and when I threw open the door of the room, my chair was empty. I drank a small straight whisky and got myself to bed.

CHAPTER 10

THERE WAS A BOAT away to the west of us with one man in it. He was fishing. The boat was drifting broadside on before the very light westerly breeze, and he was casting from it. There was a gleam of clouded sun, and I could just see the intermittent flash of his rod as it whipped over his head.

I nodded in his direction. "Don't see many boats," I said. "Can anyone fish here?"

Mr. Callender took his eyes off the drifting boat and turned to me. He was smiling his usual small smile, but the look in his eyes did not quite go with it. "We can't stop people fishing from the shore," he said. "That's if they're prepared to walk to the water, which most of them aren't. But you can't put a boat on the water unless you own a bit of shore. There's several who do, of course. I don't know who that would be." He turned back to watch the boat again. He watched it very intently, but the fisherman was still some way away and took no notice of us. He crouched in the stern of his drifting boat, intent on the path of his fly across the dappled water.

"He's got good weather for it," I said. Mr. Callender nodded but said nothing. For obvious reasons I was in no position to cross-examine him on the point, but I had very little doubt that he didn't know much about boats and fishing and was not very much interested in them. This seemed odd for a man who chose to live in a place like this. I supposed it was the choice of Mrs. Callender, who did and was. She, after all, was here much more than he was.

We motored on towards the north shore, crossing the line of the fisherman's drift when he was still quite a long way west of us. When we came in under the landing stage, Mr. Callender got off carefully on to the steps and stood there. He had an oilskin neatly folded over his arm, but I thought that as soon as he was up the bank it would be flung into the boot of the car or perhaps left hanging in the garage. In his neat dark suit he would look much more at home in his big car than he ever would in a boat. For just a moment he hesitated. I wondered if he was going to tell me when he would be back, so that I could meet him with the boat. Instead he said, "Oh—get back as quick as you can, will you? I think my wife has something she wants you to do."

I was pleased at the prospect of seeing Mrs. Callender when I got back, but even so I was not completely happy about the way he said it. He spoke easily enough, but the touch was missing. There was something on his mind, and I wondered what it was. I suppose I connected it with Mrs. Callender. At any rate something quite indefinable warned me to be careful. I put on my cheerful subordinate's smile and said, "Right. I'll get back straight away." He nodded and went up the steps. He was still preoccupied about something.

I backed the boat out and turned for home. The fisherman's boat had drifted almost on to my course now, and I wondered, in a not very urgent sort of way, which side of him I should go. Then as I looked I saw him wind in his reel. There was no fish on the line, and he did it with a sort of systematic slowness, as if he was packing up for the day. He got the line in, settled his rod in the bows of the boat and turned his attention to the outboard motor clamped on the transom. He was going home, and might by the look of it be off before I got at all close to him. But the engine would not start. He pulled once, twice and a third time. Then, being no doubt an experienced hand, he stopped pulling at it and began to look for possible causes of the trouble.

Outboards have a reputation for unreliability which does very little justice to their perennial and extraordinary efficiency in the most adverse conditions. What is true is that when, like any other engine, they occasionally fail, they are apt to do it at awkward moments. But here there was no sort of crisis. The boat continued to drift lazily, as it had no doubt been drifting for a couple of hours past, across the huge sheet of faintly ruffled water. The engine would start presently, and the fisherman would have lost only a few minutes on the long haul back to wherever he had come from. He set about the engine with the patient thoroughness of the man who knows what he is doing and has plenty of time to do it. If I held on course now, I was going to pass very close to him. Etiquette demanded at least an offer of help, even though he looked perfectly capable of helping himself. He heard my motor when I was still some way from him. He looked at me for a moment and then went back to what he was doing. When I came up with him, he had the plug out and was working gingerly on the spark gap with a handkerchief and a small tool of sorts. I cut the engine and drifted alongside. "Anything I can do?" I said.

He raised his head and looked at me. He had a lean, brown purposeful face under his fisherman's hat, and he seemed to look me over with very great thoroughness. Then he smiled slightly and shook his head. "I don't think so, thank you," he said. "She'll be away presently, I don't doubt. And I'm not in any great hurry."

I said, "All right, so long as you're sure."

"Ah, I'll be all right." He took his eyes off the plug and gave me another of those very penetrating stares. "You'll be working for Mr. Callender?" he said. "New, though, aren't you?"

"Quite new. I've only been here a few days."

"Is that so? And what happened to the chap that was here before? What was his name, now?"

"Mackie," I said, "or so I'm told. I never met him."

"Did you not, now? Gone before you came, was he?"

"That's right. Went very suddenly, Mr. Callender said. I don't know why."

He was leaning out over the stern of his boat now, gingerly screwing the plug back into the cylinder head. He did not take his eyes off what he was doing. He said, "When would that be, then?"

"I don't know," I said. "All I know is that he was gone before I got here. Mr. Callender was needing someone and offered me the job."

He put the lead back on the plug, straightened the engine up and began to wind the starter cord round the fly-wheel. Then he sat back and looked at me again. "And where do you come from?" he said.

There was no mistaking the interest. And there was something else I was now suddenly aware of. What had been a casual conversation had become something much more like an interrogation; and he was a man used to asking questions. So far as I knew, I was not in breach of the criminal law, but I was nevertheless not anxious to be interrogated. I gave him back stare for stare. "From the south," I said.

He did not seem at all put out by this. I think he even smiled a little. He did not seem at all hostile, merely interested. He said, "Mr. Callender was lucky to find you, then. How did you get in touch with him?"

I smiled back at him. "Pure chance," I said.

"Chance?" he said. "You met Mr. Callender by chance?" He looked carefully at the starter cord wound round the fly-wheel, though there was nothing about it that wanted looking at. He said, "You didn't know Mackie at all?"

"I've told you," I said, "I never saw him."

"And you don't know what became of him?"

I shook my head. "Only that he left here," I said.

He looked at me for a moment in doubt. Then he nodded and, turning round, pulled the starter cord. The engine started noisily and he had way on the boat at once. He raised a hand palm forward and waved as he went, heading away westward. I watched him go a little way and then turned to my engine. As it started, I remembered Mr. Callender's instructions to get back as quickly as possible. I could not have wasted more than a few minutes, but I felt vaguely guilty. As I headed south, I turned and looked over my shoulder towards the landing stage on the north shore. It was some way behind now, and my glance was a hurried one. I could not swear to what I thought I saw. But I thought something moved on the top of the bank above the landing stage. I straightened the boat on course and then turned round for a better look. I looked long and carefully. I still do not know whether I had imagined it, but there was nothing there now.

I put the boat on the beach under the jetty and went straight up to the house. As I came on to the terrace, I saw George come from the back of the house. I imagined he had come from the powerhouse. He saw me, but went straight in at the side door without stopping. He seemed to be in a hurry. Fifi was standing in the kitchen window, and I waved to her. When I came to the door, she was there to meet me. There was no sign of George. I said, "Good morning, Carrie. How are you this morning?"

She dropped her eyes and smiled, rather as I had seen her smile to herself over the washing up. But this time she flicked her eyes up and looked at me, still smiling, through her enormously thick lashes. "I'm fine, thank you," she said. "Did you want to see Mrs. Callender?"

"Yes, please. I gather she has a job for me."

"Oh? Well, I'll tell her you're here. George is with her now."

"All right," I said. "You do that."

She went off along the passage, and I stood at the door for quite a time, wondering what all the urgency was about. I expected Fifi to come back, but suddenly there was Mrs. Callender coming towards me. She had on what I thought was a linen dress in some very pale color. In any case, the soft, rather heavy stuff clung to her as she moved. She seemed to light up the dark passage. Her eyes were very wide open and fixed on me as she came. I didn't think I could ever be tired of simply watching her.

She said, "Thank you for coming up. Did my husband tell you?"

"He said you had a job for me, yes."

"Yes. Well, it's out here. Will you come?"

I stood aside and she led me round to the back of the house. She went straight to the door of the shed I had come out of barely twelve hours before. Then she turned and looked at me. "In here," she said. I think I spent a good part of the rest of the morning trying to remember and interpret the look on her face, but in the end I had to give it up. The face itself was almost completely without expression, but there was something in the eyes or the voice, amusement, indignation, even a trace of anger —I could not tell. It may have been all in my own mind.

I looked at her with polite interest, but my mouth was a little dry. "After you," I said. She opened the door and went in, and I went in after her. The shed was nearly full of packing materials. There were boxes and cartons, bundles of corrugated cardboard, straw, shavings, paper of every kind. I looked it all over carefully before I let my eyes come round to the mound of filled sacks at my left elbow. I knew exactly where to look, but I do not really think there was anything much to show. There was a dent, but it might have been anything. Then I looked at her. "Very inflammable," I said. "What do you want me to do?"

"Clear it all out," she said. "I want the shed clear. Keep the whole sacks and anything in the way of wooden boxes that's really worth saving. All the rest you can burn. Only down-wind and well clear of the house."

"I'll do that."

"Good." She turned and went past me to the door. In the doorway she stopped. "Was there a boat out on the water just now?" she said. "I thought I saw one. One doesn't often."

"Yes. Fisherman. Your husband was saying that you can't put a boat on the water unless you own land on the shore."

"That's right. I wonder who it was? What was he like, this man?"

"Oh—lean-faced, rather sharp-eyed chap. Quite pleasant-spoken."

"You spoke to him?"

"Yes. Not for long. His engine wouldn't start, and I had to ask him if I could help."

"Did he want help?" All this time she was standing in the doorway of the shed, looking out towards the back of the house. I stood behind her, inside the shed. She made a breathtaking picture, framed in the dark doorway, but the smell of sacking and tarred stuff was very strong and reminded me of the evening before. I was in a state of fair mental confusion. I suddenly found this irritating. I wanted above anything else to shake her out of her icebound composure.

"No," I said, "he didn't need help. He asked about Mackie."

I could not say that she showed surprise at this, but at least she stopped talking half over her shoulder, as if she was just on her way back to the house. Instead she turned and faced me again. She was still only just inside the doorway, but she had her back to the light. "Did he know Mackie?" she said.

"I'm not quite sure, now I come to think of it. He must know him by sight, because he knew I wasn't him. He recognized me as a new face and asked what had become of Mackie."

"And what did you say?"

"What I knew. I don't know much. I said Mackie had left suddenly and was gone before I got here. The job was going and your husband offered it to me. That's right, isn't it?"

"Quite right. What did he say to that, this fisherman?"

For the second time that morning I suddenly found myself being systematically questioned, and I reacted in the same way. I said, "He didn't say much." Her head went up at that, as if she felt my resistance. For a moment no one said anything. We simply stood staring at each other, though she could see me much better than I could see her. Then I said, "Why did Mackie go, in fact?"

I had more than half expected her to be angry, but instead she lowered her head again and looked at me under her eyebrows. The attitude was almost submissive, and when she spoke, she spoke very softly. "Does it matter?" she said.

"I think I'd like to know. At least I'd know what to avoid."

She said, "That's what I'm afraid of." As I have said, I could not see her face very clearly, but from the sound of her voice I suspected the quick flicker of a smile I had seen once or twice before. She only did it when her head was down; it went with the upward look under the eyebrows. It was very uncharacteristic, and disturbing in proportion. I never failed to respond. Now I said, a little breathlessly, "What am I supposed to understand by that?"

She was quite serious again, but her voice was still soft. "Oh—there was a row," she said. "There was trouble between him and

James. He couldn't stay after that."

"So James— So your husband got rid of him?"

She said, "I got rid of him." She said it very quietly, but the effect was extraordinarily chilling. It was difficult to say why, except that there was a sense of finality in it and no trace of compunction. It reminded me of a farmer whose dog had been caught worrying sheep. A pity, but no alternative. It was only afterwards that the comparison struck me as odd, but I still had no doubt about it.

All I said was, "That seems to make it more than ever necessary that I should know what to avoid."

"I'll tell you what to avoid when you come to it. You've only got to do what I say." She suddenly came across to me, there in the dark shed, with the dented sacks at our elbows, and put her hands on my shoulders, as she had once before. It is not a thing a woman usually does. It came naturally from her because of her height and the whole feeling there was about her of physical equality. "Will you do what I say?" she said. "You will, won't you?"

I put my hands round her. I did not try to pull her close to me. What I wanted was to make it clear, I suppose to her, certainly to myself, that the thing was in balance. I said, "That would be up to you, I think. I have very little doubt you could make me if you wanted to." That was true, but I was consciously very slightly surprised at myself, even as I said it, for seeing it so clearly.

"Could I?" she said. "I'll have to try, then."

She smiled at me, a very deliberate, concentrated smile this time. I knew, as I had known the first time I saw her, that a full smile did not become her. It overemphasized the slightly harsh line of her mouth. Then she tried to draw away from me, but I held her where she was. She pushed against me with both hands, and then, when this did no good, dropped her hands suddenly on to my arms just below the elbow, trying to break my grip. It was almost a wrestler's trick, and she did it with startling force. When she found my arms still round her, her eyes opened very wide and stared into mine. I could not tell what was in them. I was smiling myself now. I pulled her close against me, leaving her arms where they were, caught between us. Then she gave way all at once. Her eyes closed as her face turned up, and we kissed with a sort of concentrated violence.

I had been quite wrong in thinking that one or the other of us would have to be drunk before I could make love to Mrs. Callender. There would be no difficulty at all. But this was neither the time nor the place for it. The point had been made, and I myself broke off the kiss and held her away from me.

"You do that," I said. But I was almost as breathless as I had been when I came out of the cold water. "Now I'll get on and clear this stuff, shall I?"

She nodded, but did not say anything. She was looking at me with a sort of surprised calculation, as if she was seeing me for the first time. Then she turned and went out of the shed. I gathered a load of straw and paper and went out to look for a suitable place for a fire. When I had dumped the stuff I looked out northward towards the invisible landing stage. I wondered how far along the line the fisherman's drifting boat had crossed it. It would be quite some way. A glass would have picked it up easily enough, but hardly a casual glance of the naked eye. I wondered why Mrs. Callender should have had a glass out, but I did not know the answer.

CHAPTER 11

I HEARD the sound of the outboard in the almost windless morning and immediately connected it with the idea of my keen-eyed fisherman. I went outside to look, but there was no boat in sight. The sound was coming from under the eastern side of the island, against what breeze there was. I think I had it in mind to see him again if I could. My original resentment at his questioning had been overlaid by the uneasy conviction that both Mr. and Mrs. Callender had made it their business to watch our meeting.

All this time the sense of escape had filled my mind to the exclusion of almost everything but casual and intermittent excitement. The only thing I was afraid of was the intolerable world I had got away from. The island life was paradise enough, even without its excitements, simply because it was not London and Ashwood. It was about now I began to wonder about it. Looking back, I think the moment had been when Mrs. Callender, standing in the doorway of the shed, had questioned me too closely about my chance encounter with the fisherman. The possibility that there was, after all, no escape, that I had only exchanged one sort of tyranny for another, was now at least a thing that might need looking into. I was not yet worried about it. As Mr. Callender had said, I only had to ask. Only, as he had also said, I was by way of having burned my boats, and did not see offhand where else there was for me to go.

But I didn't want to go anywhere else yet. I had kissed Mrs. Callender after I had answered her questions. I was full of curiosity, but there was still only one thing I immediately wanted. I walked slowly down the path towards the jetty. All the time the sound of the motor got louder, but there was still no boat in sight. Then, quite suddenly because it was quite close inshore, it came round the shoulder of the island, and I saw that it was not my fisherman at all, but our boat with Mrs. Callender and George in it. They had evidently come round from the slip under the powerhouse, and now, as I watched them, they headed northward away from the island. I thought I could see fishing gear in the boat, and Mrs. Callender, sitting on the forward thwart, was bent over something she had in her hands. I pictured her putting her rod together or tying on her cast. Whatever it was, she concentrated on what she was doing. George, at the outboard, looked only ahead. Neither of them looked at me. I stood there on the path and watched them going away from me.

I did not want them to see me watching them. George was not likely to, but Mrs. Callender might at any moment raise her eyes from whatever she was doing. I turned and started walking up the path. Then on an impulse I turned again and looked at Mrs. Callender. She still had not seen me. I dropped into the heather beside the path and lay there waiting for the boat to get well away before I put my head up. When I looked again, they must have been a couple of hundred yards out from shore and had turned westward. They were both looking ahead now. Mrs. Callender still had not got her line out, though I thought I could see the rod resting on the stem of the boat. The whole thing looked very purposeful. I wondered if they were looking for my fisherman of the day before, but I could see no boat anywhere to the west. At any rate, they were not thinking about me. I got up and ran up the path and into the cottage.

The breakfast things were where I had left them in the sink, half washed up. I was going to finish them, but thought better of it. I could do that any time. I went outside again. The cottage was between me and the boat, but the sound of the motor came faintly on the gently moving air. It sounded very far away now. I went up the path towards the house. No one could see me here. I thought Fifi was probably somewhere up at the house, but even she could not see me until I came over the shoulder of the slope. I had just got my head over the crest when I saw movement at the side of the house, and stopped. A moment later Fifi came out on to the edge of the terrace. She was facing in my direction, but I didn't think she could have seen me. At this time yesterday I should have gone up to meet her, but at the moment that was not what I wanted. I dodged back down the path and then turned off it. I ran a matter of ten yards and took cover behind a rock. The slope was full of them, lichen-coated outcrops of granite thrusting up out of the heather. I had no very clear purpose in this, except that with George and Mrs. Callender out of the way I wanted to be on my own. I could see Fifi later. Unless the boat came back unexpectedly soon, there would be plenty of time for that.

I lay there in the heather, watching the crest of the path. For what seemed quite a long time nothing happened. Then Fifi came over the crest, heading down the path. She was going quite slowly, almost sauntering, as if she too didn't know what she was at. I thought she was smiling slightly to herself, as she had smiled over the washing up. I wondered whether she would go to the cottage or merely past it. She might even be going to the empty cottage. I wondered, if she was looking for me, what she would do when she found no one at home. Go back to the house ultimately, of course. But not quite at once. Unless I had got her very wrong, she would be unable to resist the temptation to have a look round in my absence. She would be wanting to know more about me, over and above the curiously intimate and superficial knowledge she already had. So far as I was concerned, she was welcome to spend as long as she liked exploring. There was nothing of me in the cottage, only the new clothes I had bought at Duncastle with Mr. Callender's fifty pounds. I had some exploring of my own to do. I knew what I wanted now.

The moment I was sure she could not see me, I got up from behind my rock and went straight up the slope towards the house. Over the shoulder of the slope I picked up the path again, and after that I ran. The side door was shut but not locked. Unlike me, Fifi had finished the breakfast washing up before she sallied out to do whatever it was she was smiling at as she went down the path. The kitchen was tidy and empty. It had the dry warmth and faint, not unpleasant scent of food which all well-kept kitchens have. But I had already seen the kitchen from outside the window, and I wasted no time on it. The passage ran straight to the back of the central hall, which it met at right angles. As you went along the hall towards the front door, you had, as I had thought, the dining room on your left and the sitting room on your right. The stairs went up the east side of the hall. The sitting-room door was open. I went in and stood in the middle of it, taking it all in. It was quite a pleasant, ordinary room, except that there were no flowers anywhere. There were books, a lot of them new, tidily packed on built-in shelves. They had the sort of elaborate, middle-of-the-road catholicity which suggests the book-club selection rather than any one person's taste. The pictures were the same. If anyone in the household brought you into a room like that, you would accept it without a thought. Seen like this, surreptitiously, as part of an empty house, it had undeniably the feel of a stage set. I went to the big front window and looked out. The terrace cut out the part of the path immediately below it, but I could see the path where it went over the shoulder of the hill and the roof of the empty cottage. I could not see Fifi anywhere. I went out into the hall, listened for a moment and then ran upstairs.

The stairs turned back on themselves and went up the west wall to a corridor that ran the length of the house. There were rooms opening off it on both sides and one at its western end, over the kitchen. There was no window in the corridor, but there was a glazed skylight at the head of the stairs. All the doors were shut. I turned left and went along the corridor to its western end. I walked quickly, but on tiptoe. I cannot think what good this silence was likely to do me, but it was instinctive. I was still, on the whole, enjoying myself. I opened the door and went into a perfectly empty room. There was a window in the wall opposite me. This would be the one over the kitchen window, which I had considered from out on the terrace a couple of evenings before. No wonder it had been dark then. There was in fact a small single bulb hanging from a flex in the middle of the ceiling, but I doubt if anyone ever switched it on. The room was not only unoccupied and apparently unused; it was completely unfurnished. It had not even had anything dumped in it. There was a very thin layer of dust on the floor, as if the room was given a routine cleaning at intervals and was now about due for one. There was nothing else at all.

I found this disconcerting. In a house that is permanently lived in, a totally unused room is very rare. The temptation to put things somewhere is too strong. But beyond the disconcerting fact itself there was nothing to keep me. I shut the door quietly, went back along the corridor and opened the first door on my left. It was furnished as a single bedroom, and had a window looking out over the water to the north shore. From this floor you could see a good deal more of the slope down to the jetty, but there were still patches of dead ground. Almost the whole height of my own cottage was clear of the intervening curve of land, but it was masked by the empty cottage above it. There was still no sign of Fifi. The room was so tidy and characterless that I thought of it immediately as a spare room, though the bed was made up and there was a pair of men's hairbrushes on the dressing table. I opened a cupboard and found two suits hanging in it, both dark, apparently exactly similar. This was George's room. Perhaps mainly a dressing room. I was not speculating at this stage. But the whole thing was as elaborately unrevealing as the man himself, and I wasted no more time on it.

The next room on the right was recognizable as Fifi's before I had so much as got the door ajar. I suppose it was the scent, though I had not thought of her as using anything identifiable. Once I had got the door properly open the thing was even more obvious. The room had frilly touches and was only superficially tidy. The coverlet was stretched tight over what I suspected was a rather badly made bed. There was nothing lying about, but when I pulled open a drawer under the dressing table, a confusion of silky clothes bulged out of it, so that I had to force them back with one hand while I shut the drawer with the other. The clothes were all perfectly clean. It was like the way Fifi herself broke out of her clothes when you took the pressure off them. There was something rather endearing about it. The window faced out over the outbuildings and across the top of the island to the powerhouse. There was much less to look at, but it would get the sun. I had no doubt Fifi would prefer it. It was a servant's room, all the same.

The bathroom was adequate but not luxurious. The top of the window was open, and I peered out of it in case there was any sign of Fifi, but I saw nothing. The remaining south-facing room was a man's room, but much less bleak and uncommunicative than George's. The single suit and the odd jacket hanging in the cupboard had been made by a proper tailor, and the top drawer of the dressing table had a neat stack of white handkerchiefs, good linen and carefully laundered. There were even a few books. But it was not a room a man lived in. The odd thing was that it did not suggest so much the week-end cottage as the sort of room a busy man who can afford it keeps in town, to use on occasions when his engagements do not allow him to get back to his home thirty or forty miles out. It went very well with Mr. Callender's style, but left a lot of questions unanswered.

I knew of course that the remaining room at the front of the house must be Mrs. Callender's, but in any case it was unmistakable. I had never known a woman's bedroom with less scent about it. It was not Spartan at all. The dressing-table gear was elaborate and fairly expensive, but it was designed to keep Mrs. Callender as she was, not to embellish her or cover her up. There was a full range of clothes from what she wore under her fishing gear to what looked like evenings or nothing. I remembered Mr. Callender saying, "You'll not be needing a dinner jacket on Carney." If Mrs. Callender had evening clothes here, it was because this was where she lived and she had nowhere else to put them. The bed looked comfortable to the point of luxury, and was a bit bigger than the beds in the other three rooms. It remained a single bed. Four single beds in four separate rooms, each highly characteristic of its occupant. For a house occupied by a husband and wife with another couple looking after them, it was, to say the least of it, an unusual arrangement.

All this took really very little time indeed. I did not spend more than a matter of seconds in each room, and I almost ran, always on tiptoe, from one room to the other. When I looked out of Mrs. Callender's window, I saw Fifi coming up the path. She was quite near the house, but the edge of the terrace would still be between her and the side door. I ran downstairs two at a time, regardless of the noise I made, and went along the passage towards the kitchen. I noticed as I went that there were two doors in the left-hand wall, but I had no time to open them. One, I knew, was the small bare room I had dumped the stores in when I brought them up from the boat. I did not know what the other was, but it would keep. I went out of the door, shut it quietly behind me and dodged left round the back of the house.

I was in time, but only just. Fifi's head had not appeared over the terrace when I got outside, but I had been no more than a second or two round the corner of the house when I heard her heels clacking over the paved path leading to the side door. I ought to have made some effort at pretense in case she came round the corner and found me, but I was so certain that she would go into the house that in fact I did nothing. She went in, all right. I heard her feet pause and then the door shut behind her. I gave her a few minutes in case it occurred to her to make sure that I was not in the house. I imagined her running upstairs, as I had, and putting her head into each door in turn. But she may have done nothing of the sort. After a minute or two I walked casually round to the side door. Not having hard heels, I could not make as much noise as she had on the path, but I made what I could. Nothing happened.

I opened the door, went inside and put my head into the kitchen. Fifi was at the sink again, washing something out in a basin. I think it was the tea towels. She was really very domesticated and thorough, and I liked her for it. She heard me come in and turned her head over her shoulder to look at me without taking her hands out of her basin of suds. She looked startled, but there was a good deal of the ineradicable archness in it. She was not really worried about anything. Bent over the sink like that, she looked even nicer from behind than she had from in front. She turned back to what she was doing, but now she was smiling her small smile over it. "Where have you been?" she said.

I gave the standard reply. "Looking for you," I said. "I couldn't make anyone hear, so I went round the back. Then I heard you come in." I did not want her to consider this too closely. I went up to her, put my hand on her shoulders and ran it down to explore the soft curve humped over the edge of the sink. She went on with her washing as long as she could, and that was pretty surprisingly long. Even then she rinsed her hands methodically under the cold tap and dried them on a towel over the draining board before she turned and clung to me, with her face turned down, while my hand went on doing what it was doing. If she had had any doubts about where I had been, she had forgotten them. So, for the matter of that, had I. We were both desperately preoccupied. After another minute or two she suddenly dug her fingers into me, and there were a few seconds of violent agitation.

She raised a pair of clouded eyes to me, and as they cleared gave me her little smile. "What about you?" she said.

"I'll keep," I said. I did not want to talk to her any more now. I kissed her quickly once and went outside and down the path. I was beginning to worry about what I had seen upstairs.

CHAPTER 12

I FOUND one of the long drawers of my dressing table shut with a tag end of shirt tail sticking out at the top. This was a thing I could not do myself. It would give me a feeling of discomfort, as if it was my own finger caught in the drawer. I concluded that Fifi had, as I supposed, found the cottage empty and had a quick ferret round it. I wondered whether I had left any similar trace of my exploration at the house. At least I had not left any clothes sticking out of drawers. I remembered pushing Fifi's own bulging clothes back into her drawer and the trouble I had had with them. But ten to one, if I had, she would not have noticed anything unusual.

And the truth is, I didn't mind about Fifi. I think it was because I could not imagine myself in any circumstances being afraid of her. I knew very little about her, but I thought I knew the sort of person she was. There may be, in any physical relationship between a man and a woman, a moment of truth when the barriers go down and the mental relationship changes irrevocably. Getting very drunk with a man may have much the same effect. I am not saying for a moment that every man knows the truth about every woman he has ever made love to. The woman may not surrender herself in this way, or she may surrender herself and the man be too preoccupied or too obtuse to recognize the surrender. Or he may simply not be interested. But it can happen, and with Fifi it had.

Mrs. Callender was a very different kettle of fish. I found it difficult to imagine her surrendering much of herself in any relationship; and even if the truth emerged, I doubted whether it would be any less frightening than the picture of her which, rightly or wrongly, I already had. I thought I could be frightened of George, too. Mr. Callender I was still uncertain of. There was something in him I liked, and the thing might go either way. But I could not see myself getting very drunk with either of them.

In any case, it was obviously an odd set-up I had got myself into, but I still did not think the oddness was any concern of mine. Mr. Callender had said that if I wanted to get out, I had only to ask. And of course on balance I still had not the least wish to get out. I was much too well placed where I was and any alternative I could imagine was much too daunting. All the same, I was puzzled and intrigued. Just occasionally I was disturbed, but on balance I was still firmly set on exploring the possibilities of the situation.

I suppose it was because I was curious about things that I found myself wondering about the second door on the side of the passage opposite the kitchen. It was now the only room in the house I had not seen, and I could not think what sort of room it might be. There was very little space between the passage and the back of the house, and the room where I had dumped the stores must occupy quite a large part of it. Even that was a long narrow room, with a single window in the back wall of the house. I tried to think if there was any second window beside it. I couldn't remember seeing one, but it was a thing that could easily be verified, even if I had no chance of getting at the door itself. I suppose the explanation was obvious enough, but at this point it had not occurred to me.

I was at the cottage when I heard the outboard again, as I had been when the boat went out. It was still a long way away, but what breeze there was was from the west, and sounds travel very easily over a flat surface of water. I could see nothing out of the kitchen window, but I went outside to look. I still saw nothing until I went some way up the hill, and then I picked out the boat away to the west, with the late afternoon light behind it. From what I could see, it was heading straight back to the south side of the island where the slip was. I wished I had a glass of some sort, but I had none of my own, and I could hardly pretend I needed one for my work. I thought they had glasses of some sort up at the house, but I hadn't seen any. It occurred to me that George and Mrs. Callender might have them with them in the boat, and might even now be using them. I did not want to be seen, even at that distance, standing on the slope and gazing at the approaching boat. I went down to the cottage again, but I was restless and full of unspecified expectation. I suppose the episode at the kitchen sink had in fact left me more keyed up than I was prepared to admit. I stood in the window listening to the sound of the motor because it was bringing Mrs. Callender back to the island.

After a bit the sound died down suddenly, though I could still just hear it. The boat had gone under the south side of the island. It was only when it stopped altogether that I knew they had come ashore. Then there was nothing to listen to and nothing to do. I wanted to go up to the house, but I could think of no good reason for going. I already had the feeling that I had to have a good reason for anything I did on the island. It was never my job to start anything. I just had to be there when I was wanted. If Mrs. Callender wanted me, she knew where to find me. I had never been in this position with any woman before, and I found it a very uneasy experience.

I pottered about until the afternoon turned to evening and the light began to go. Then at last I said to hell with it. I gave myself a stiffish drink and set about getting my supper. I had no clear intention in my head, but I do not think anything could have prevented me, once it got fully dark, from going up to the house to see what there was to be seen. I knew it was not possible to go straight for what I wanted, but I was set mentally on a collision course, and had no intention of getting off it. Only it takes two to made a collision. I could make my own terms with Mrs. Callender once I got within arm's length of her, but whenever I had got within arm's length of her so far, it had always been her doing, not mine. As far as I could see at the moment, this was the way it was likely to go on. I found the fact that she would have to come to me, and that I believed she would, itself a stimulus that did not make waiting any easier.

When I had finished all I could find to do, I turned on the lamp in the sitting room. This made it look almost completely dark outside, but I knew it would not really be dark for some time yet. The daylight died very hard in these parts. I drew the curtains, sat down in my usual chair and looked at my watch. I gave myself half an hour. I did not want to read or smoke. I just sat there, with my elbows on the arms of the chair and my chin on my hands, waiting for the time to pass. When I had waited twenty-five minutes, I got up, drew the curtains and looked out of the window. I could see nothing, not even how dark it was. I went back and turned out the lamp. Then I groped my way back to the window, letting my eyes get used to the darkness. It was pretty dark outside now, though there was still this gray, translucent quality in the darkness that suggested a remote source of light away to the north, which I could not see. I had said half an hour, and half an hour it would be. I drew the curtain across the window again, got back to my chair and switched on the lamp. This had occupied nearly two minutes of the remaining five. I was unable to think of anything but the time. I looked at the second hand of my watch. I saw it go twice round its dial and start out on its third round. Then the front door of the cottage opened and shut, and there were footsteps in the hall. It was all quite brisk and businesslike and made a certain amount of noise. There was nothing stealthy or cautious about it at all. The door of the sitting room opened and Mrs. Callender came in. She shut the door behind her. She had some sort of raincoat draped round her shoulders like a cloak, but as she came in, she took it off and threw it over the back of a chair. She was wearing a white, long-sleeved blouse buttoned high to the neck and a black skirt. Her hair was piled on top of her head. I had never seen it like that before. She looked dressed up for the evening. I got up out of my chair and we stood facing each other in the lamplight. I felt curiously hollow, and could feel my heart thumping against my ribs.

She said, "My husband is coming in the morning. Will you meet him at the landing stage, please? About nine o'clock."

I am not quite sure which of us had moved. Perhaps we both had. At any rate we were now quite close to each other. With her hair piled up like that she seemed taller than I was. Her hands hung loosely at her sides. She had no bag or anything. I put my hands up, quite slowly, as if I was hypnotized, and undid the top button of her blouse, under her throat. "How do you know?" I said. We were both speaking quite quietly, in matter-of-fact voices.

She said, "That was the arrangement."

I undid two more buttons. She did not move at all. "You make very careful arrangements," I said. "But you never tell me in advance what you want me to do." When I put my finger inside her blouse to deal with the next button, I found it was between the tops of her breasts.

She said, "You always do what I want when the time comes."

I undid the last button, jerked the bottom of the blouse from inside the waistband of her skirt and put it back over her shoulders. She was wearing a brassiere under it. It did what was required of it, but concealed very little. She put her arms behind her, shuffled the sleeves of the blouse off them and let it fall on the floor behind her. I put my hands to the shoulder straps and at the same time she reached up behind her and slipped the hooks. Then her arms came forward again and I pulled the brassiere forward and down. I said, "So long as I know when the time has come." I did not touch her more than was incidental to taking her clothes off. I had seen all this before, but only at a distance. It was utterly perfect, like a fifth-century statue, but warm. I could feel the warmth even when I was not touching her.

She stood there, with only her black skirt on, looking me quite calmly in the eye. She said, "You shouldn't have much doubt about that, surely." Her tone was still purely conversational, but she gave me the little quick flicker of a smile that was her most disarming expression.

"No?" I said. "No, I suppose not." I undid the hook at the side of her skirt, slid down the zip and pulled the skirt down. Whatever she was wearing under it came down with it. She was not wearing stockings, and there was none of the complicated support gear that goes with them. She moved herself enough to let the skirt go down to her ankles, but she did not step out of it. I stood there, quite close to her but still not touching her, contemplating in detail what must be the most beautiful thing I had ever seen. I still felt hollow and rather breathless, but curiously calm and tremendously happy. Then, quite suddenly, but still with the same purposeful deliberation, she leaned forward a little and began to undo the front of my trousers. For a second or two I stood there, holding my breath and feeling her fingers moving on me. Then the whole scene exploded into action.

There was, as I had thought, no surrender at all. In this, as in so much else, this marvelously made woman had the mental attitudes of a man. Like the male adept, she retained, even in the height of the storm, a consciously creative control over the whole proceeding, and exercised it equally for the benefit of both partners. To me it was a totally new experience. I think it might not have been to everybody's taste. I found it extraordinarily exhilarating.

When there was nothing more to be had, we lay side by side, full of a shared admiration and a sort of immense physical friendliness. But underneath, hardly skin-deep inside our well-matched bodies, the mental reserves were quite untouched. I knew no more what sort of person she was than I had when she first came into my lamplit room and threw her raincoat over the nearest chair. But it did not worry me in the least.

Presently she got up and went through into the sitting room, and I followed her, still unwilling to take my eyes off her, even while she dressed. She must have done her hair up with the same all-embracing efficiency, because it was surprisingly little out of order. Whatever was wrong with it she felt for and put right by touch. I had a glass in the bathroom, but she did not go to it. She was looking at me all this time. She was still friendly, but the speculation had come back into her eyes. She was sizing me up again, though I could not imagine what there was left to size me up for. The silence was kept up, I think quite deliberately, by both of us. We had the same instinct, at least in relation to each other, to let the physical side look after itself and not confuse the issue with the unexplored hazards of too close mental contact. I thought this was a masculine thing too. It is certainly a thing most women resent and break down if they can, often with very bad results.

Finally she said, "Well." We smiled at each other, it was so nicely done. The monosyllable covered everything that had happened since she had said what, according to the rules of the game as we played it, she had really come down to the cottage to say. "You'll be there at nine, then?"

"I will," I said. I bowed slightly, like a superior servant accepting an order from his master. She picked up the raincoat and flung it round her. The action of putting on a cloak is always dramatic, and the effect was quite magnificent. But it remained entirely uncalculated. She took her physical perfection for granted and expected you to do the same. She was in every respect the antithesis of Fifi, who waved her nice little body at you the whole time in case you should miss anything.

"Good," she said. She nodded and went to the door. I did not go with her. She shut the door of the sitting room behind her and marched through the hall. A moment later the front door shut with what almost amounted to a bang. The cottage was suddenly very empty and I thought I had better get properly to bed. But I did not doubt that she would be back.

CHAPTER 13

I SAID, "Have you come from the south?" and was doubtful whether I should have asked the question the moment I had asked it. Mr. Callender seemed doubtful too. It broke, even if in a very small way, the unstated rule that I should never initiate anything. I should have waited for him to tell me where he had come from. If he wanted to, that is. As it was, his eyebrows went up, and for quite a long time he considered the thing. Then he nodded. The nod was mainly to himself, as if he had decided what to do, but it also served as a partial answer to my question.

"I have come from London," he said. We looked at each other. I was not sure whether my initiative had gone far enough, and he would now tell me what I wanted to know, or whether he expected me, now that I had started the thing, to ask further questions. He was quite aware of my hesitation, and evidently decided that there was no purpose in leaving it to me. He said, "Your disappearance from the scene is known, of course, but I get the impression that no one's taking much of an interest—not after the first day or two."

"What about the police?"

He seemed surprised at that. "The police?" he said. "Ah, I shouldn't think so. You didn't go off with the Association's funds or anything, after all."

I laughed. It all seemed unbelievably remote. "No one would get far with those funds," I said. "Our credit didn't go much beyond the petty cash. But I thought—surely, if someone just disappears, the police are told."

"Ah," he said, "that of course. But once they find nothing criminal's involved, there's nothing they want to do about it. Nothing they can do, in fact. I suppose by now you're registered somewhere as a missing person, but they won't have the squad cars out looking for you. Why should they? They have probably concluded that you had your own reasons for going off. As, indeed, you had."

"What about the Turk's Head? I wondered— Someone might have heard something. Or seen me go off with you, or something."

"They might, I suppose, yes. But I don't think they did. Or if they did, they don't remember it. It's the sort of thing a police investigation might turn up. It's amazing what people will remember if you ask the right questions. But no one's asking any, so they don't. No, I've no evidence at all that anyone associates you with me in any way." He paused, and looked out across the water towards the island. When he spoke, I knew he was choosing his words very carefully. He said, "No one knows where you are at all."

That was what I had wanted to hear. It was odd and unreasonable that when I did hear it, I should have had this momentary twinge of disquiet. There was so much here, and since last night more than ever, to make this new world the world of my dreams, that the completeness and irrevocability of my surrender to it should not have worried me. When I looked at the thing with a calculating eye, in fact, it did not. There was no single thing in the old world I regretted, at least on any reasonable balance. Except perhaps one or two animals, and these were no responsibility of mine. There were no animals on the island at all, apart from the minute, invisible wild life of the place, not so much as a cat. Just the four or five human creatures permutating among themselves, coupling and uncoupling, against the vast background of sky and water. I liked cats, and the right sort of cat would enjoy it here. I must ask whether I could import one. But I must ask. That was the point, and my mind came round full circle and focused itself on the back of Mr. Callender's head, up in the bows of the boat. If he did not mind my having a cat, he would bring it with him the next time he came, or the red-faced man would bring it in his van to the landing stage and I should go and collect it. I only had to ask.

I do not know how long I took to revolve all this in my head, but there must have been a noticeable silence, because Mr. Callender turned suddenly and looked at me. I had the feeling that he had said what he had said so deliberately that he wanted some observable reaction to it. When I said nothing, he wanted to know why, and to know what, if anything, I was thinking. Out of pure perversity, or perhaps from an instinctive caginess, I told him what I was thinking. I said, "I was wondering if I might have a cat."

If I had wanted to surprise him, I certainly succeeded. His eyebrows shot up, and for a moment he looked at me with a perplexity that had a faint touch of suspicion in it. Then he seemed to shrug it off and gave me his warmest smile. "A cat?" he said. "I don't see why not."

I smiled back at him. "It needn't be a special cat," I said.

"Lonely?" he said. He said it very blandly.

"Not particularly. I just like cats."

He nodded. "Well, I don't see why not," he said again. He turned back to look at the island, and I looked at the back of his neck. I seemed to see him in a different light nearly every time I met him. The change was never of his making. In himself I do not think he changed at all the whole time. It was other people who changed round him. It was odd that he should have asked me, on this morning of all mornings, whether I was lonely; but then I had never asked him for a cat before.

Now that I came to think of it, I thought that my answer to his question had not been quite true. The truth was that I was lonely, but did not at the moment mind. I suppose the picture of myself as a lonely man with two mistresses on a pint-sized island tickled my vanity. But then my vanity, so long lost and now so suddenly rediscovered, was still a thing to be indulged in with almost conscious enjoyment. For a man, as for a woman, this kind of physical vanity is one of the purest and most secure pleasures. So long, of course, as the physical grounds for it remain. I did not want Mr. Callender to stay on the island very long, but for the moment I liked having him. I wanted very badly to see him and Mrs. Callender together, or I suppose, more correctly, to see Mrs. Callender in his presence. This was a thing which in fact very seldom happened. I wondered if I could find any way of contriving it, but offhand couldn't see any.

When we got ashore he said, "There's quite a lot of stuff that will be going back with me tomorrow. I want to get off pretty early. If you'd like to get it down this evening, I'll see it's ready, and you can get it stowed overnight. You can put a tarpaulin over it. But it won't hurt, most of it, even if it does get a bit wet. Not that it's bound to rain, but we'll be lucky if it doesn't. Will you do that?"

"I will," I said. I expected him to give me a time, but he did not. I was on the point of asking him, but stopped myself. I saw it at once as an excuse to go up to the house, and the more freedom I was left with it, the better. He nodded and went off up the path, walking sedately in his dark suit with his briefcase in his hand. He looked for all the world like a man walking from a suburban station to his detached house in its bit of garden with a few of the original hedgerow trees still standing at the bottom of it. And to his educated, civilized suburban wife. The huge emptiness he walked through did not suit him. It suited Mrs. Callender. Whether she was educated I had no means of knowing. I doubted whether I should call her civilized. At any rate, I watched him walk up the hill towards her. Whatever happened when they met, I should not be there to see it.

I saw nothing of them all that day. I very seldom did when Mr. Callender was on the island. Inevitably, I did what every man does, one way or another, once he has made himself a married woman's lover, I tried to imagine them together—tried to, or occasionally tried not to, but in any case went on imagining it. I did not do it at all clearly. I could not see her responding to, or even wanting, the warmth I still felt in him, and I could not see him measuring up to her ruthless and all-pervading physical efficiency. If I got to know her better, as it was presumably in the cards I might, I might well come at a better understanding of him through her. It would not be the first time this had happened. In the meantime I found them, as a couple, not at all easy to understand.

I went up to the house after tea and got to the side door without seeing anyone. I looked fairly carefully into the kitchen window as I went past it, but could see no one inside. I knocked on the door. I knocked loud enough to establish my good faith, but not loud enough to rouse the house if everybody was at the far end of it. Nothing happened and no one came. I opened the door and went into the passage, leaving the door open behind me. The obvious thing in the circumstances was to look into the room on the right, and this I did. There were half a dozen cases ready packed there. They made, as Mr. Callender had said, quite a load, though they would not be beyond the capacity of his big car if he was traveling by himself. I came out into the passage again, shutting the door after me, and stood there, listening. There seemed to be people talking somewhere in the house, but the voices were very faint and intermittent. I thought they might even be coming from upstairs. The one risk, obviously, was that someone should come to the side door behind me, but it was a risk I had to take. It would not do to shut it. I went back to the door and looked outside. There was no one about. Even if there was someone about at the back of the house, it would take him a few seconds to get to the side door, and a few seconds was all I needed. I went back inside, went straight down the passage and tried the second door on the right. It was not locked. I opened it quietly and put my head inside.

There was nothing but a small square space. A single bulb hung from the ceiling, but there was no window. The whole of the left side was occupied by a second door, at right angles to the one I was looking through. It was shut. It was a perfectly ordinary door, but someone had fitted a heavy staple and hasp to it. There was a padlock hanging on the staple. It was an ordinary label lock, of the kind you can buy anywhere, but fairly formidable. It all looked much newer than the door, as if it had been fitted only very recently. I did not touch anything. I backed out into the passage, shutting the door quietly behind me. For what it was worth, I had the answer now. It was one I might have thought of before. The inner door could lead to nothing but stairs. There was no room for anything else. These would be the cellar stairs, and the cellar, obviously, was where the deep freeze was. It would have to be a pretty large affair, and there was nowhere else for it to be.

A door opened somewhere, and the voices I had heard were suddenly quite loud and close at hand. I backed step by step to the side door and almost through it. Then I stood where I was, half in and half out, trying to look as if I had just opened the door from outside. I put on an expression of hesitant inquiry and waited for someone to turn up. I waited so long that I felt my face freezing into a sort of desperate immobility, and the muscles of my leg began to complain as I leaned forward in the doorway. Then Fifi appeared at the far end of the passage. Her eyes snapped open as she saw me, but she did not smile at all. I could make nothing of her expression, except that it was one I had not seen before. I had the sudden conviction that I was seeing the real Fifi for the first time, but before I could bring the idea into focus, Mrs. Callender appeared behind her. They walked towards me, these two women I knew everything and nothing about, one behind the other, and I did not know which pair of eyes I ought to be meeting.

I had in fact no choice. Mrs. Callender was more than a head taller, and I do not think any man could have found himself face to face with her and not looked at her. She smiled at me suddenly, a small, quick, familiar smile. As if under compulsion I smiled back at her as she came towards me, but all the time I was conscious of Fifi's eyes watching me from just below the direct line of my vision. I was not very clear in my mind about anything, but I know it was all very uncomfortable. Then Fifi turned right into the kitchen and Mrs. Callender came on alone. All this time none of us had said anything. Then I swallowed and said, "I've come— I think there's some stuff to go down. I knocked, but couldn't make anyone hear."

She ignored the last bit altogether. She said, "Yes, that's right, it's in here." She opened the door on her left and went in. I followed her. She was looking at the stuff, not me, and I did not have to go through an act of seeing it for the first time. "James said— I think there are one or two more things to come, but this is most of it. Can you manage it?"

I was standing behind her and very close to her, because there was no room to stand anywhere else. "I'll do my best," I said. The words were almost completely meaningless, but I spoke them softly and within an inch or two of that hanging cloud of silver-gilt hair, which smelt of nothing but herself. If she had turned her head sharply, the hair would have brushed my face, but in fact her face came round slowly, and she must have shifted her ground a little as she turned, because when we faced each other, our heads were not as close as they had been. But they were close enough. She gave me once more that quick, flickering smile.

"You do that," she said. "No one could ask for more." For a moment or two I looked at her, surprised, as I think at that stage of an affair a man often is surprised, by the speed and completeness with which my desire had returned to me. She did not move. She simply looked back at me, but she was no longer smiling. It was for me to move first. I stepped back into the passage and stood aside for her. She went past me into the house, and as she went we bowed very slightly to each other. Nothing more was said. I lost her footsteps on a carpet somewhere in the house, and there was complete silence everywhere. The kitchen door was shut. I looked at it for a moment and then went into the storeroom and picked up the first two boxes. I put them down outside and came back and shut both doors. Then I picked them up again and set off along the side of the house and down the path. I did not look into the kitchen window as I went past it.

I made three journeys of the stuff already there, and before I came up for the last of it, someone had added one more case, which meant a fourth. It was a quiet, silver-gray evening, and I took the job comfortably. I was at ease with myself and full of a sort of peaceful exhilaration. The first time I had done this up-and-down porterage, Fifi had been waiting for me at the cottage, with a bottle of whisky in her hand, when I came up for the last time. All that seemed to belong to a different age which was now quite difficult to understand. When I came up for the last case, Mrs. Callender was standing in the almost empty room, looking at it. She turned as I came in. "I'm afraid this one's rather heavy," she said.

I went past her to the case, and when I turned to face her, with the case between us, she was standing in the doorway. I stooped over it, feeling for the best handhold, and she stood there looking down at me. She said, "I don't want you to take too much out of yourself." Quite suddenly she smiled her full smile, showing the white even line of her perfect teeth. I suppose it was precisely because this smile did not suit her that it laid her defenses open as nothing else did. As long as it lasted, she was human and vulnerable, partly because of the feeling that lay behind it and partly because she had for the moment ceased to look her best. There were footsteps in the passage beside her, and she turned, still smiling that wide smile, to whoever it was coming up on her left. Then she turned to face me again and Mr. Callender appeared beside her in the doorway.

The expression on her face had not changed at all. She had somehow included him in the smile, so that now he was smiling too. They stood there together in the doorway, both smiling down at me. For the fraction of a second I stared up into the two smiles. They were the same smiles, that was the point. Whatever I meant to either of them, I meant the same to both. I swung the case up on to my shoulder and went forward with it. They stood back, and I went past them with the bulk of the case between my head and theirs. I went out of the door with it and down the path. The whole world had turned suddenly cold, and I went in a daze, wondering where I was and what I was going to do next.

CHAPTER 14

I LAY AWAKE for some time after I got to bed, thinking about Mr. Callender's smile. But my evening exercise up and down the path had had its effect. At some point still fairly early in the night I must suddenly have turned over and gone to sleep, and after that I slept quite heavily. When I woke, the disquiet of the night had receded to the back of my mind. The front of my mind was filled with Mrs. Callender. Whatever had been in Mr. Callender's mind when he had stood there in the doorway, he would be gone again by early this morning, and Mrs. Callender would be free, if she wished, to come down to the cottage in the evening. I thought she would wish to, for all Mr. Callender's smiling.

A breeze got up with daylight, blowing as always from the west, and stiffening as the morning went on. It brought the cloud up with it. The whole world was much less attractive. When I took Mr. Callender and his cases across to the landing stage, there was a short, sharp sea moving across our course, and he needed an oilskin over his town clothes. Otherwise everything was exactly as usual. We did not in fact say very much, but what little was said had no overtones. When we got under the lee of the stage, I made the boat fast while he went up to unlock the garage and get his car out. Then I carried the cases up. The heavy one, having been last stowed, went up first. As I picked it up, I remembered very vividly the two smiles I had faced over the top of it, but when I brought it to the gaping rear of the big utility, Mr. Callender was entirely concerned with getting it in without damaging anything. He need not have worried. You could have put a coffin, at least a coffin for a man of medium height, in that car and not made more than a temporary dent in the thick haircord on the floor.

I stowed the other cases round it, and we both stood for a moment looking at them. Then he reached up to shut down the back flap. I went over to shut the garage door. I thought he was going to say something when I made the move, but if he had been, he thought better of it. The door was heavy but beautifully balanced. The locking mechanism must have been built into the body of the door, because nothing showed on the inside, but when I swung it down, it locked with a heavy click. I did not think anything except the proper key in the lock would have much effect on it. The key was in Mr. Callender's pocket, but I should have been surprised if it was not a pretty thorough piece of precision steelwork. When I turned round, he was standing by the driving door of the car. I said, "All secure." He nodded and got into the car.

"Right," he said. "I'll be back about this time the day after tomorrow."

"I'll be here," I said. But mainly I was wondering why he was giving me my orders now. He had never done it before. I remembered saying to Mrs. Callender, "You never tell me in advance what you want me to do," but I had said it with my fingers inside her blouse and between the tops of her breasts. I had not expected her to remember it, let alone pass it on to her husband. But the thing could be pure chance. He started the car and backed her slowly on the turning circle in front of the garage. Then he raised a hand and was off.

I went down to the boat and then, as an afterthought, went up the steps again and walked round the outside of the garage. It was, as I had thought, of the same school as the powerhouse, heavy stonework, with barred windows high up in the walls and a flat roof. A good secure job, with no expense spared. When I got back to the boat, the steady westerly invited a straight reach home, and with a light ship it seemed too good to miss. I ran the sails up under the lee of the stage, pushed her head round and then, as she pulled out into the wind, let the centerboard half down. She leaned over stiffly and lumbered off over the gray moving water, while I sat with my back to the wind, holding the tiller and sheet and trying to pretend we were going twice as fast as we were. From the house on the top of the island Mrs. Callender might or might not be watching my progress, but for the moment I was perfectly happy where I was. I simply pointed her at the island and then, without altering course, pulled the centerboard up at the last moment and sailed straight up on to the beach.

When I got into the cottage, I was met at the door by a current of chilly air blowing in from the other side of the house. I knew what it was, and swore. The bathroom window had blown open. The bathroom was at the far end of the hall. Its window faced west, and its top half consisted of a hinged flap with a spring catch which never locked properly. When the wind was hard in the west, I kept it wedged with a fold of paper, but now it was some time since we had had any wind to speak of, and the damned flap had blown in again. One of these days it would break its glass doing it, but for the moment it was hanging there as usual, intact, but letting the wind blow straight in. I shut it crossly and put the wedge in place to hold it. Then I went out of the side door and round to the back of the cottage to have another look at the weather.

Unless I was mistaken, there was some nasty weather on the way. The sky to the west was darkening all the time, and the wind came in repetitive gusts from under it. The rain would reach us in an hour or two, and then it would really blow. I looked at the cottage sitting there, with only the one window facing the prevailing wind, and wondered why, when the builder had been so sensible, the joiner could not have made a better job of it. Just up the hill the empty cottage turned an identical back to the wind. I suppose it was this that gave me the idea. I went out on to the path and looked up it. There was no one about. I turned in at the gate of the empty cottage, went straight round to the back, doubled my fist with a handkerchief round it and gave the top of the bathroom window a controlled but hearty thump. It succeeded almost too well. The flap flew in with a bang, and for a moment I was afraid I might have broken the glass. But it was all right. I stood on the cement lip of the gulley, where the bathwater ran out at the bottom of the wall, and put my head and shoulders into what had been Mackie's cottage.

It had the smell of an empty house, but only very slight. I knew it was kept dusted and aired, because I had once seen Fifi at it. In any case, I did not believe it had been empty very long. Unless I was much mistaken, the furniture had been moved down into the lower cottage only just in time for my arrival. When Mackie had really left I still did not know. I put my hands on the glazing bar at the bottom of the opening and heaved my top half inside. The window was over the bath, not the washbasin, and there was no great difficulty in the maneuver. I lowered myself forward head-first until I got my hands on the edge of the bath. Then I wriggled my legs in one after the other and finished up sprawled across the bath. There was a spider running frantically round in the bottom of it. I picked him up carefully and put him outside. I am fond of spiders in a respectful sort of way, and I doubted if he would get anything like the same consideration from Fifi, even if he survived until her next visit. I shut the top flap of the window. It fastened better than mine did, and would stand up to the wind, if not to a punching fist. Then I tiptoed into the empty cottage.

I do not know what I expected to find. I suppose something that might help to satisfy my curiosity about the vanished Mackie. There was in fact nothing to see. There was nothing movable anywhere. I had another look at the sunbleach marks on the wall that I had seen through the front window, but learned nothing from them that I didn't already know. The light was very bad now for the time of day, and the smaller details were difficult to see. I was getting nowhere, and I thought I might as well go back the way I had come. It was just as I was having a last look round the sittingroom that I saw a light fleck on the floor and stooped to look at it. There was a thin coat of dust over everything, but I blew this off. A small wedge-shaped splinter of wood was gone from the end of one of the floor boards. The boards were stained, and the natural wood showed up clearly where the bit was missing. There was a single short length of board here, nailed to only three joists, and the break was next to one of the end nail holes. I looked at the end of the board itself and saw what I had expected to see. Someone had put in something like a cold chisel or wrecking bar and prised the board up off the joists. It was the only short length in the whole room, and if anyone was interested in prising up floor boards, this was the one to go for. The board had been nailed firmly back, and I had nothing but a penknife on me, but now that I knew the way in, the thing would keep.

I went quickly over the floors of the other rooms. None of them had any likely boards except the bedroom, which had a short section in one corner. I got down on my hands and knees and looked at it very carefully. Nothing was broken here, but the board had been taken up. Whoever had put it back had been an enthusiastic amateur, and had hammered the wood round the nailheads in a way the builder's carpenter would never have done. This put a different complexion on the thing, and I confirmed it when I found signs of tampering on the lining of the wall cupboard on the other side of the kitchen. No second visit was called for. There was no treasure under the floor after all. There may have been, and somebody at some point had certainly thought there might be. But if it had ever been there, it would not be there now. Someone had gone over the stripped house with something a good deal cruder than a fine-tooth comb. I wondered what it was that Mackie had had of his employers' that they had been at such pains to try to recover after his departure. The impression I had been allowed to gather of the cause of dispute between Mackie and Mr. Callender no longer seemed very probable. Whatever Mackie might be suspected of hiding under the floor, it was certainly not his mistress's favors. But I thought I knew now why the lower cottage had been so hastily brought into use for my benefit. If the Callenders could not find what they were looking for, they wanted to make certain no one else did. I thought for a moment what a happy irony it would be if Mackie had, as I had, found his way into the empty cottage and hidden whatever it was there. But I doubted, after all, whether this possibility would have been overlooked. I had just come to this conclusion, with my head still in the kitchen cupboard, when somebody put a key in the lock and opened the front door.

There was, finally and absolutely, nothing I could do. The kitchen opened only into the hall, and whoever it was was already in the hall. I could not get back into the bathroom, even if it would have been possible to clamber out of the bathroom window again without being heard all over the cottage, which it almost certainly would not. The side door of the cottage opened out of the kitchen, but the door was locked and the key had been taken away. The feet in the hall went into the sitting room, and I partly shut the cupboard and retreated behind the open kitchen door. There for the moment the thing hung. I did not think I had left any marks of my exploration that would be visible in the now very murky light. No one would know I was there unless they actually saw me. With the bathroom window firmly shut, it was on the face of it impossible that anyone should be in the cottage at all. There was just the remotest chance that I might get along the hall and out of the front door without being seen or heard, but it was very remote indeed.

The feet came out of the sitting room into the hall, but went back to the front door again. For a moment I believed that they were going altogether, but while I was still holding my breath they came back again, and something was put down with a faintly metallic bump on the sitting-room floor. There were further, softer sounds that were at once familiar, and suddenly the whole thing added up and I knew the answer. I still wanted to get away with it if I could, but I minded much less. The moment the vacuum cleaner opened up, I tiptoed out from behind the kitchen door and into the hall. At the same moment Fifi, I still do not know why, came out of the sitting-room door. It was the reverse of our original collision in the hall of the other cottage. It was different from it in every sort of way.

She let out a high yelping scream and shrank against the wall with the back of one hand against her teeth. Even in moments of the greatest stress she still did everything in character. I could not blame her for being startled. I must have looked very large and dark emerging into the dusky hall like that, and there should not by rights have been anyone in the house at all. I did not want to frighten her unnecessarily. I stood where I was, smiling at her, so that she should have a chance to recognize me and get her wits back. Her hand came slowly down from her mouth, but her mouth was still slightly open and she panted a little.

I would have bet any money you liked on her opening line, but I should have been wrong. I thought she would say, "What are you doing here?" and I knew that not even I, this time, could get away with saying that I had come to see her. When she did speak, it was in little more than a whisper, and with the vacuum cleaner still droning away behind her I could scarcely make out the words at all. She said, "No. Oh, no."

There was a sort of incredulous horror in it that turned my stomach. There was something here I did not understand, and I suddenly felt much less sure of the whole situation. I said, "Turn that damned thing off, for God's sake."

She nodded. The wall plug was on the baseboard just inside the sitting-room door. She stooped and put a hand down, and the thing stopped on a dying note. She hardly took her eyes off me as she did it. Then she straightened up again, standing where she was by the side of the doorway. We made no move towards each other at all. With the vacuum cleaner stopped, I could hear that the wind was getting up outside. It whispered and rustled on the roof and walls and every now and then raised its voice and moaned slightly. It was very dark now. I spoke only just loud enough to make myself heard against that stealthy background of sound. "No what?" I said. "I was only having a look round."

She was still staring at me as if something about me horrified her almost beyond her powers of expression. She said, "But why? I can't—" She suddenly caught her breath at something in her own mind. "Did you know Mackie?" she said.

"Mackie?" I said. "Of course I didn't know Mackie. How should I? I never set eyes on him."

She seemed to find this confusing rather than reassuring. She passed a hand across her forehead and shook her head slightly. Like so much else she did, it had the look of a stereotyped stage gesture, but there was no mistaking the sort of nightmare confusion that lay behind it. She shook her head again. "I don't know," she said. "I thought—"

I went up to her in that whispering darkness and took her very gently by the shoulders. She made no move either towards me or away from me. She just stood there, with her hands hanging at her sides, looking up at me. I said, "Carrie, tell me one thing. Why do you all sleep in separate rooms up there?" I jerked my head in the direction of the house.

She answered straight away, but listlessly, in a small toneless voice, like a person talking in her sleep. She said, "We sleep separately because we're not—because we're separate people. I mean—"

"But you're married to George, aren't you?"

She roused herself suddenly, and the fear came back into her eyes. She said, "I'm not supposed to—" Then she put her hands up and beat them on the front of my jacket. "No, no, no," she said. "I'm not married to George, and I don't sleep with him. Please, please believe that. I oughtn't to tell you, only I don't want you to think—"

I said, "All right, all right, Carrie. I believe you. I don't understand it, but I believe you. What about Mr. and Mrs. Callender, then?"

She was calmer now. "I don't know," she said. "It's always been like that. I don't think Mr. Callender— I've heard George go into her room at night sometimes, but not Mr. Callender. Only I don't know what he went for. I don't know if they slept together. They may have just wanted to talk." Her eyes turned away from me sideways and downward. She seemed to be trying to work something out. Then they came up again. "How do you know?" she said.

"Know what?"

"Know that we all sleep in separate rooms. Have you been over the house?"

I smiled down at her, trying to make light of it. "Only when I couldn't find you," I said. "I couldn't make anyone hear, so I went upstairs to see if there was anyone there."

I felt her fingers close on the lapels of my jacket. "You mustn't," she said. "You mustn't explore like that. They don't like it. It's not safe. The house is bad enough, but the powerhouse is the worst. Promise me you won't go to the powerhouse. That's what—" She caught her breath and looked at me doubtfully.

I finished the sentence for her. "That's what Mackie did," I said. "Is that it? That's what Mackie did. He tried to find out things, so they got rid of him. Isn't that right?"

She caught her underlip in her teeth and stared up at me. Her eyes were wide open and looked almost luminous in the dark hall. She nodded but said nothing. Then she clutched me with a sort of desperation. "Go away," she said. "Please go. Please, please go."

I patted her reassuringly, though God knows I had very little assurance left in me. "All right, all right," I said, "I'm going. If you'll let me out of the front door—"

She did not move, but gripped me harder than ever. I think she even shook me a little, like a mother losing patience with a child who refuses to understand. "I don't mean just out of here," she said. "I mean right away. Get away altogether, while you still can." She paused, staring up at me. Then she shook me again. "Oh, please, please," she said.

I stared down at her, and for the first time fear, a conscious cold fear of the whole damned place, crept into the back of my mind. I would not let her see it. I still smiled at her as best I could. I said, "Let me out of here to start with, anyhow." She let me go, and I went to the front door and opened it. For the time of day it was outrageously dark outside. It was blowing really hard now, and the rain had started. I turned up the collar of my jacket and ran for the shelter of my own cottage.

CHAPTER 15

It never stopped blowing most of the day, and at intervals the rain came with it, hurling itself at the back of the cottage and sounding as hard as hail. I stayed indoors all the morning, because there was nothing that could be done outside and, as far as I knew, nothing that needed doing. It was not a very enjoyable morning. I was in a torment of uncertainty. My instinct was to go away, as Fifi had told me to, but I knew no solid reason why I should, and in another part of my mind I did not at all want to go.

Whichever way I tried to think, my mind grounded on ignorance. For one thing, I didn't know how much notice I ought to take of Fifi. I did not for a moment believe that she herself knew all the facts. Whatever George was, she was certainly in some real sense my fellow servant, not one of the management. And apart from that, everything she did made it very difficult to take anything she said quite seriously. In the first respect I was, as I know now, right. In the second I was wrong. But I could not know this at the time. All I knew for certain then was Ashwood and what going back to it would involve. It would need an immediate and unmistakable menace to make me face that, and at the moment the menace was very ill-defined. More than that, it seemed to depend on what I did. So long as I was content not to interfere with whatever was going on, no one, as far as I could see, had any reason to interfere with me.

Something was going on, obviously. Whatever they were doing, the Callenders were not there for the fishing. But whatever it was, I was not involved in it, and could afford not to notice what didn't concern me. In the meantime, my life there still had its compensations. At this stage I was as much unable to face leaving Mrs. Callender as I was to face returning to Ashwood. All the same, I was curious. Also, precisely in so far as I did not know, I was uneasy, and however I argued the thing, the uneasiness would not quite go. The truth is, Fifi had frightened me, and I could not get it completely out of my mind.

By the middle of the afternoon I had to get out of the house. The wind had dropped by then, though I did not think we had by any means seen the last of it. All I wanted was to walk, and I turned westward along the north side of the island. It occurred to me before I had gone very far that I had turned that way because there was nothing there. I was already acting, even unconsciously, on Fifi's warning not to seem to be exploring, and I did not like it. Whatever happened now, the peace had gone out of my escape, and only the adventure was left. The adventure was still real and compelling, but it was not primarily what I had been after when I had made my escape. I wondered whether a man like me, lacking what Jock Galbraith called the cutting edge, carried his own servitude and insecurity around with him, however far and fast he ran away from reality.

I came out on the western end of the island above the beach where I had watched Mrs. Callender undress and later swum with her in that disastrously cold water. That was an intrusion which apparently did not matter. I had been right, even then, to think that any sort of intrusion on the privacy of her body was less important than one on the privacy of her mind. I had been given friendly access to the body now, but the mind was as inaccessible as ever, and seemed at times hostile in its inaccessibility.

Not even Mrs. Callender would swim for pleasure today. The gray water broke in a short repetitive flurry of white on the steep beach, and the wind, though well down now, had all the coldness of the water in it. I went on along the edge of the island, following the indentations of the shore and losing my sense of direction in the process, until I suddenly found that I was facing east again and that the powerhouse was straight ahead of me. I had never seen it from this side before, and I was seeing it from almost the level of the roof, whereas before I had come on it from below. There were complications above and behind it, between the end of the roof and the slope of the island, which I had not noticed. The power went to the house on overhead lines carried on not very high poles, but this hardly accounted for all the metalwork I could see.

I think it was because I had started by subconsciously avoiding it that I now, consciously and determinedly, examined the whole thing carefully from where I stood. Then I went down the slope towards it, until its top came up against the sky in front of me. Then I stopped dead. There was a sudden jolt of reminiscence, a moment of bewilderment and then a clear but surprising association. There was nothing here really at all like the great steel spider's web I had seen against the evening sky on my way up with Mr. Callender, but one had reminded me of the other, and once my mind had made the connection, it went on working on it. I had asked Mr. Callender what the spider's web was, and he had said the Americans. He had not explained it further.

Something moved by the north end of the powerhouse, and I dropped on my knees and crouched in the wet heather. I thought I had been caught doing just what I had been forbidden to do, and I was suddenly and comprehensively frightened. I waited, head down, holding my breath, and then, when nothing happened, lifted my head slowly and peered over the curve of the heather in front of me. It was George, of course. He was moving about between the powerhouse and the slip. I thought he was making sure that the boat was fast. Like me, he expected it to blow up again in the night. I watched him for perhaps a quarter of a minute, ducking when he seemed likely to turn my way. When I put my head up for the last time, he had his back almost towards me and had started up the path towards the house. He had something under his arm. It looked like a folder or portfolio. At any rate it was flat, the sort of thing that holds papers or nothing. I waited until he disappeared over the curve of the path. Then I got up and ran back the way I had come.

By the time I got to the cottage the wind had gone almost completely, but the sky was still heavily overcast, and it was going to get dark early. I went to the writing table. I had paper and envelopes there, which I had not touched since I came. I did not know how I was going to get a letter away, even now, but I had to try. I addressed an envelope to Jock Galbraith at the bank address which had found him before. Then I pulled out a sheet of paper, dated it and simply started writing. I wrote, "*Dear Jock, This may be all moonshine, but I'd rather give it to you than not.*" I stopped and listened for a moment to the silence. Then I started writing again. I had a tremendous sense of urgency, even though I did not know at all what I was going to do with the letter when I had written it.

When I had finished it, I sealed it in the addressed envelope. By now it was almost completely dark outside, and I had already turned the light on. I drew the curtains securely and then picked up the envelope and wondered where to put it. I had a sudden picture of Mackie, his face a blank because I didn't know what he looked like, down in the other cottage looking for somewhere to hide a paper; and of George, after Mackie had gone, taking up floorboards and tearing the place apart trying to find it. I put the envelope in the inside pocket of my jacket. Then I went to the door and put my head outside. It was dark and very quiet, only somewhere there was a faint continuous noise in the air. I walked to the edge of the bank and listened. For a little nothing changed, and then suddenly the sound, though still very faint, grew momentarily stronger, and I knew what it was. Somewhere out on the water, not so very far out, there was an outboard motor running. It was just turning over and probably four-stroking. It sounded very stealthy.

I had no time to confirm this, but I never for a moment doubted that it was not George's boat from the powerhouse slip. The only other boat I had seen was the fisherman's, and as things now were I very badly wanted to see him again. I turned and ran back to the cottage, picked up a torch from beside my bed and ran back to the top of the bank. The sound was more definite now. I thought the boat was moving eastward along the north side of the island, but keeping well out. I waited, fingering my torch, for the sound to come opposite me. Then it stopped altogether.

It occurred to me afterwards that if the boatman was coming ashore, he would certainly at some point have cut his motor and taken to his oars. But at the moment all I felt was that I had lost touch with him and must somehow re-establish contact. I pointed the torch out to where the sound had last come from, and had just put my finger on the button when I heard someone coming down the path behind me. I put the torch back in my pocket and scrambled as quietly as I could down the bank to the edge of the water. I crouched there, listening, and heard precisely nothing. For quite a time nothing happened, and then from out on the dark water there came a muffled wooden sound. It was the sort of sound which a man moving about in a small boat may make by accident, and which carries astonishingly across flat water. Almost at once the footsteps moved again on the path behind me, and there was a metallic click.

I knelt on the heather, put the torch against my stomach and spread my jacket forward on both sides to mask it. I looked over my shoulder, prayed that my Boy Scout's Morse would not fail me and flashed three words very slowly in the direction of the invisible boat. I flashed DANGER KEEP OUT. I waited for a bit and then flashed it again. For quite a long time nothing happened. Then from some way out there came the unmistakable splutter of a starting engine. I heard the engine turning over again, very faintly, at intervals after that, but it got fainter and fainter until I lost it altogether. Whoever it was, and whether or not he had read my warning, he had gone. I was alone again on the island, with my letter to Jock Galbraith in my pocket and someone with something that clicked on the path behind me.

For a moment or two I knelt there, wondering what to do. Then from over the water a puff of cold air blew suddenly and a second or two later another came after it. The wind was coming back, as I had thought it would. The heather began to rustle all round me and there was a ruffle of water on the beach. I started to move, as quietly as I could, but by now not greatly caring whether anyone heard me or not. The cottage was dark when I got back to it. I let myself in and turned all the lights on. I saw no one and heard nothing but the wind all the way.

CHAPTER 16

I THINK the mere writing of my letter to Jock Galbraith must have eased my mind, even though I still did not know how I could get it away to him. I slept soon after I got to bed. By then it was blowing steadily again from the west, and by morning it was as bad as it had been the day before. I slept late and was woken by the rain drumming on the roof and window. The sort of temporary assurance I had achieved by writing to Jock had vanished, and I was right back in the unresolved contradictions of yesterday.

The only hope of settling anything seemed to rest with Fifi. Whatever else was true, I knew she was frightened of something, or her fear would not have communicated itself to me. I wished now that I had got more out of her when I had had her alone in the cottage, but I had been infected with her panic and the instinct to get out had been very strong. Now it seemed the only thing was to get hold of her again and make her tell me what she knew. There was no other possible source of information. Wherever the line was drawn, and whatever line it was, Fifi and I were on one side of it and George and Mrs. Callender on the other.

At the moment I could not go even if I made up my mind to

do it. The boat was down there on the beach, still with the fuel in her which I had saved by sailing back the day before, and indeed with the sails themselves. But I had seen enough of the seaway between here and the north shore with only a steady breeze blowing to know what it would be like now. She was a stout old boat, and built for it, and might batter her way through, but it would not be nice. If I got to the shore, there would be nothing but a howling wilderness, howling all too literally, and an unknown length of private road between me and what must be one of the remoter edges of the outside world. And even then I did not know where to go. It seemed a very desperate venture to undertake on the strength of an unexplained panic on Fifi's part and a completely unverified suspicion on mine.

By the time I had got myself some breakfast, the rain had almost stopped, though it was still blowing as hard as ever. It would be very wet underfoot. I put on ankle boots and a zipper jacket and went out into the wind. I walked straight into it, heading westward along the slope of the island, out of sight of the house. When I had gone a couple of hundred yards, I turned off in a long left-handed curve until I reckoned I was pretty well due west of the house. This was the only reasonably safe angle of approach by daylight. The terrace on which the house was built unsighted most of the ground-floor windows for some way round it. It was the upper windows I had to worry about. Only one of these faced west. That was the window of the empty room, and I could think of no reason why anyone, on this day of all days, should be keeping a lookout there. In any case, now that the rain had stopped, there was nothing intrinsically improbable or suspicious about my coming up to the house by the western slope, and if I was seen, I should not have much explaining to do. Once I got near the house, I could move up from behind the outbuildings until I was within yards of the side door and the kitchen window.

I turned and began to walk up the slope. The blank window of the empty room stared down at me. I thought if there was anyone there, I could probably see them, and I saw nothing. I walked slowly, leaning my weight against the gusts that hurled themselves at my back. The whole sky was covered with a continuous sheet of driving gray cloud, and as far as I could see in every direction the black water rolled eastward under it in steep menacing lines breaking in bursts of white. It lacked the strength and scale of the sea, but I reckoned it would swamp an open boat in next to no time. I came to the top of the slope, moved slightly across to the right and had the outbuildings between me and the house. Then I stopped. I had come up, driven on by the wind and my own disquiet, without any very clear plan of action. I could not stay there long, in case I had been seen, but I needed to take stock and have an opening gambit ready, whether it was Fifi I met or one of the others. I was full of apprehension again, moving consciously into enemy territory. I gathered my wits and my breath and went on along the side of the shed I had been in before. I had just got to the end of it, near the corner of the house, when I heard a man's voice shouting some way off to the right, beyond the backs of the other buildings.

The wind carried the voice away from me, and I could not hear what he was saying, but the shouts were repetitive and urgent. The one thing I knew was that it could not be me he was shouting at, because no one in that direction could have seen me. I suppose it was the certainty I had not been seen that made me do what I did. I opened the door of the shed and dived inside. I pulled the door shut after me until there was only a crack left to look through. Then I stood there with my eye to the crack, waiting.

A moment later George ran past the shed and made for the

side door of the house. He had stopped shouting now, but I could hear him fighting for breath as he went past. He was wet almost from head to foot, so wet that the water splashed off him as he ran. It must have been cold work, running about in the wind as wet as that. Merely being out in the rain would not have done it. He had been in the water. Trouble with the boat, I thought. I remembered the boat pulled up on its slip under the powerhouse, and wondered what things would be like there with this wind blowing.

Then George came running back along the side of the house and a moment later Mrs. Callender came after him. She was wearing a big white duffel coat with a hood and heavy sleeves. I had never seen her in anything the least bit like it before, and it struck me as extraordinary gear to be wearing for some sort of emergency maneuver with a small boat. The same thought must have occurred to her at the same moment, because she checked, looked at one sleeve and then turned back to the door. She threw the hood off and was unbuttoning the coat as she ran. A very few moments later she was out again. She wore only slacks and a heavy dark sweater, but carried some sort of jacket rolled in her hand. Her hair streamed in the wind. Whatever the trouble was, she showed no signs of confusion. She moved fast, but every movement was still rounded and economical, and her mouth was tight shut. I gave her time to get well clear of the outbuildings at the back of the house. Then I opened the door of my shed and came out. Mainly I was glad that George, whatever trouble he was in, had not thought of trying to get me to help him with it. If it had anything to do with the boat, I was not surprised. I was plainly meant to have nothing to do with it. In any case, I could think of very few crises of that sort which Mrs. Callender would not handle at least as well as I should, especially if it meant getting into that deadly cold water with this wind blowing.

Meanwhile the two people I wanted to avoid were down on the far side of the island, up to their necks in some sort of emergency and, from the looks of it, in cold water as well. I did not know where Fifi was, but at least I could look for her unimpeded. I went to the side door of the house. Mrs. Callender had slammed it shut after her, but it was not locked. I opened it, went inside and shut it after me. The three doors that opened on to the passage were all shut. I opened the kitchen door and put my head inside. There was no one there. The heavy white coat which Mrs. Callender had left behind lay across the kitchen table where she had thrown it. I did not touch it, but it still struck me as an odd thing for her to wear. I had the feeling that it was a garment made for some particular purpose. There was some idea niggling at the back of my mind, but I could not think what the purpose might be. I walked along the passage and into the hall. Then I stood still and listened. The noise of the wind was everywhere, but it was background noise, all outside the house. A window in one of the downstairs rooms rattled occasionally, but otherwise the silence seemed all the more oppressive because of the turmoil outside.

I was suddenly convinced that the house was empty. I started to go along the hall, but stopped at the foot of the stairs. I called, "Carrie! Carrie!" but no one answered and nothing stirred. I ran up a few stairs until my head was not far below the level of the upper landing. "Carrie!" I called again. Then I fairly shouted, "Carrie! Are you there?" Anyone who was in the house must have heard me, but still no one answered. I felt frustrated and ill at ease. I was not out for exploration today. The empty house was no good to me. I wanted Fifi, and I could not think where she could be. I went slowly back along the passage and into the kitchen. The white coat was still spread-eagled on the table. I put a hand out and felt it. It was very thick stuff, a coarse wool, very warm but shapeless and very slightly grubby.

Suddenly I had it. I think I had seen a picture somewhere, dockers unloading frozen meat from a refrigerator ship or something of the sort, with mittens and white hooded duffels draped over their working clothes. I ran out of the kitchen and opened the left-hand door on the other side of the passage. The light in the small square space was on. I went in and shut the door behind me. The door on the left was slightly open. The padlock, with the key in it, hung open on the staple and the hasp was back. I could even see a light on the far side of the door, at the top of the stairs. I pulled the door open and looked down into the cellar.

The air was chilly but fresh. There was no touch of cellar damp about it. It must have been ventilated from somewhere. I began to go down the stone stairs. As I went down the sound of the wind faded almost completely, but another sound took its place. Somewhere below me there was the muted hum of refrigeration machinery. There was a second light burning at the bottom of the stairs but no second switch. I do not like cellars, and just as I got to the bottom I had a sudden horrifying picture of someone, perhaps even in good faith, turning out the lights and locking the door at the top. I turned and tiptoed up the stairs again. I unhooked the lock from its staple and took it downstairs with me. I knew it was a silly thing to do, but I could not bear to leave it where it was. The door itself had no lock. When I got to the bottom, I put the lock on the bottom step and went on into the cellar.

It was a big cellar. It must have extended under at least half the house. It was mostly empty. There were some boxes on the far side and a line of empty bottles against the wall at the bottom of the stairs. The cellar itself was old, much older than the house. I could not be mistaken about this. The floor was partly stone flags and partly the bedrock itself, cut to a reasonable level, and for much of their height the walls were rough work of naturally weathered stones. Almost certainly they had originally been laid dry and at some time since mortared in. There must have been a house here long before the present house was built, and the cellar had been part of it. It was an uncouth place, and I did not like the feel of it.

The refrigeration plant was reassuringly ordinary. It was bricked in to almost the full height of the cellar, and there was a steel door with a long-shanked handle. It was the sort of thing you walk into. There were a couple of hooks on the brickwork at the side of the door, and a white coat like the coat upstairs was hanging on one of them. Mrs. Callender must have been getting out what she wanted when George had raised the alarm. She had shut the refrigerator door, but left everything else as it was. I pulled up the heavy handle and swung the door open. As it opened a light went on inside and a wave of enormously cold air rolled past my legs.

There was a central floor space of about three yards by two, with alleys leading off it between the shelves and racks. I have no experience of such things, but there seemed to me something rather grisly about it. Everything was there in profusion, but dead and frosted over in the dim yellow light and the breathless steel-sharp air. Much of it was boxed and packaged, but there were enormous quarters of meat hanging naked and purplish on hooks, and on one side of the floor space what I took to be the entire half of a carcass wrapped in sacking.

I edged into one of the alleys to see the extent of it, and as I did so heard footsteps on the floor above.

I think even now I was more frightened of being shut in than I was of being discovered. I whipped back into the central space, tripped over the sacking bundle and came down half across it on my hands and knees. For a second I crouched there, with the deadly cold of the floor striking up into my arms and legs and my mind blank with a sudden incredulous horror. Then I scrambled up and got myself out of the door into the cellar. The air which had seemed so chilly when I came down the stairs closed round me like a warm bath, and for a moment I hung on the door handle, fighting against the blind instinct to get out of the place as fast as I could, regardless of all caution. Gradually caution reasserted itself. I shut the door of the freezing chamber as quietly as I could and tiptoed to the bottom of the stairs. The padlock still lay on the bottom step, and I could hear no sound at all on the floor above.

Once I was on the stairs there could be no retreat. I drew a last breath of the cellar air, picked up the padlock and took the stairs at a run. The door into the passage was still shut, with the light burning inside it. I hung the lock back on the staple, shut the cellar door to the right extent and listened. The noise of the wind was back now, blurring everything. I thought I could hear movements, but very faintly, as if they came from one of the rooms upstairs. I opened the door with desperate care, listened again, heard nothing and put my head out into the passage. It was empty and everything was quiet. I shut the door behind me and began tiptoeing towards the side door of the house.

I was still not within reach of it when I suddenly heard the footsteps again, behind me and very near at hand. The side door, like all other outside doors, opened inward, and I had no hope at all of getting out of it in time. The door of the storeroom was there at my left hand, and I flung myself into it. I shut it behind me as far as I could without letting the latch click home. The footsteps came along the passage from the middle of the house and went into the kitchen. Whoever it was shut the kitchen door behind them. The one thing I wanted was to get out of the house. I peered out through the crack of my nearly shut door, wondering whether I could risk a move to the side door. Then the kitchen door opened and Mrs. Callender came out into the passage. She was wearing some sort of sandals and the white duffel coat. She had the coat bunched round her and, as far as I could tell, nothing under it. Her hair was dark with damp and hung straight down all round her head like a metal helmet. Her face was quite expressionless. She went into the door by the cellar steps and shut it after her. I came straight out into the passage, opened the side door as quietly as I could and got myself outside.

The wind hit me at once, nearly pushing me against the side of the house. For all I knew, George might be coming up from behind me and Fifi watching from some unguessed vantage point, but I simply did not care. I was off down the path, running before the roaring gusts as if I was running for my life. My only remaining purpose was to get off the island as soon as I could. I still did not know what was happening or why, but I knew that sides of butcher's meat, even frozen and wrapped in sacking, do not have toes that turn up at one end and a nose standing up from a blind muffled face at the other. I knew now where Mackie was, and I had no wish to emulate his career any further.

CHAPTER 17

THE WIND DROPPED GRADUALLY from about midday onward. I stayed in the cottage and saw no one from up at the house. If the wind was well down by dusk, I was going to take the boat and go. The water would go down with the wind. That was one of the great differences between these waters and the sea. The water got up as soon as the wind blew, like a man blowing on a saucer, but it went down just as quickly when the wind stopped. There was no ground swell, built up across miles of open sea, to keep the pot boiling. All I wanted was a reasonable breeze before it got too dark to steer any sort of course. But it was still heavily overcast, and it would get dark early. I spent the afternoon listening to the wind and watching the color of the sky. I should have liked to go down to the boat, but didn't want to be seen near her until I was ready to go. I had no reason to think I was being watched, but I could not get over the feeling that I was.

I had made no coherent plans. There were no plans to make, because I knew so little. I was going to take the boat to the north shore, leave her there and walk eastward along the private road that led to the outside world. Beyond that I could not see. What my own future might be if ever I got out of this nightmare I did not even want to consider. I wanted to take all my own things with me and leave everything that belonged to the Callenders. That seemed very important to me at the time. I could not really set off in an open boat at dusk wearing my dark office suit and my town shoes, but I got as near as I could. I put on a sweater and oilskins over my own shirt and trousers and underwear. My jacket and shoes I bundled into a canvas sail bag that belonged to the boat. The cottage still looked occupied, with the bed made up and clothes in the drawers and food in the kitchen. I even drew the curtains and turned on the lamp in the sitting room. Only this time when I left it I was not coming back.

I had no idea of the time. The only things that mattered were the wind and the light. The wind was still a lot stronger than it had been when I had come back from the north shore the day before, but it was falling all the time. I went out of the side door from the kitchen. There was an even gray light everywhere. The water didn't look too bad. It still rolled steadily eastward before the wind, but it was not too steep and was no longer breaking anywhere. I went along under the wall to the front of the cottage and looked up the path. I was out of sight of the house, but if anyone was watching the cottage, I knew that they could see me and that I had no hope of seeing them. That was just a risk I had to take.

I went back into the cottage. I told myself that I was just checking up, to make sure everything looked normal. In fact I just wanted to see it again. It had become my home, the first home of my own for a very long time, and a lot had happened there. But when I was back inside it there was nothing to see, though I looked in every room in turn. I went out through the kitchen to the side door, but this time I went out and shut it finally behind me.

The boat was where I had left her, pulled well up on the

beach in the lee of the jetty with her stern in the water. There was a lot of water in her. It was well over the floorboards in the stern, but after the rain we had had in the morning, that was to be expected. I was not going to waste time pumping her out now. I could do that once we were under way. I was going to motor, not sail. With the wind where it was, no one at the house would hear the engine, whereas on the huge sheet of gray water a sail would be sufficiently conspicuous for some time yet to attract even the casual eye. The possibility of pursuit once I was away was a thing I had not seriously reckoned with, and I did not know what the chances were. It was possible that on calm water the small boat with the outboard could go quite a lot faster than I could, but the water was still far from calm, and our course was across the seaway. I did not think the small boat could make any real speed in these conditions without great risk of capsizing. But really I did not think there was much chance, once I was away, that anyone would come after me.

I walked straight down to the boat and dropped my small bag into the bows. The wind ruffled over the top of the jetty and the water broke in small oblique waves on the beach, but nothing else stirred. The gray curve of the island hung over me, with the rocks rising out of the heather in stealthy, unfamiliar shapes, as they always did at dusk. I could have been seen from fifty different places, but I could see no one. I kept telling myself that no one knew what I had found in the cellar, no one had any reason to expect me to go. Fifi had told me to go, but I did not know where Fifi was. Nevertheless, it all seemed too easy. I had the clearest possible sense of forces arrayed against me, but I could not make out where they were or what they were doing. I could not in reason see what they could do to me once I was away, but I still could not quite bring myself to believe that they were letting me go.

I dragged the boat down until she was just afloat. The keel

grated loudly on the pebbles, but the sound went away eastward on the wind. The water in the boat looked a bit less now that it was spread more evenly over her length, but it still sloshed about over the floorboards as she rocked in the little waves under the jetty. I turned her head out, and got in over the transom, pushing her out gently as I did so. I went to the engine at once. I did not really believe it would start, but it fired at the first turn of the crank, and we moved out steadily from under the lee of the jetty.

I knew at once that I had underestimated the difficulty of the conditions, even as they were now. The little dark waves came very sharp and close together, thumping against the port topsides of the boat, and we went occasionally into a violent corkscrew roll, so that I had to turn her head into the sea to steady her. But there was plenty of freeboard, and I thought that if I took it steady, we should be all right. It occurred to me once that there was a lot of vibration in the engine, but I didn't take much notice of it. I kept the boat going steady with one hand and with the other got to work with the hand pump on the water that was washing violently backward and forward across my feet as the boat rolled. We were clear of the island now, and with any luck conditions were as bad as they were ever going to be.

We pulled steadily away from the island in the half-darkness. The engine was working well enough, but there was still a lot of drumming from the stern, especially when the boat rolled. I do not know how far we had gone when I first had doubts about the pump. I had been working away steadily to clear what I took to be the accumulated rainwater in the boat, and she should have been getting much drier by now. Only suddenly I realized she wasn't. The water still slopped heavily across the boat and over my feet, and of course it made each roll less easy to recover from than it should have been. It was not easy to see the outfall of the pump without stopping work on the plunger, but I managed it at the third attempt. The pump was drawing all right. For several seconds my mind rejected the only possible conclusion, but I think I already had it in mind before it demonstrated itself unarguably. We were taking water, not a lot, but steadily. I thought the pump was just about holding it, but if it came in any faster, we should start to fill. If she filled far enough in these conditions, she would be unmanageable in no time. I looked back towards the island. It was a long way astern now, but still just visible in the gloom. I could not see the north shore at all. The immediate physical fear of that dark, ice-cold water overcame any other fear my mind could hold, and I had no alternative. I turned her head into the seaway, came right round in a single violent roll and headed back the way I had come.

For a few seconds, while I brought her round, I had had to take my hand off the pump, but now I went back to it again, working away at it with a sort of steady desperation. I wondered if I could keep it going strongly enough until we were back on the beach, with only the one hand to spare for it while the other wrestled with the plunging, unhandy boat. Already my shoulders and arms ached dully, and I was finding it increasingly difficult to do the two things simultaneously as well as I needed to do them both if we were going to get back. All this time the vibration in the stern was building up until I began to have a monstrous apprehension that this, and the water slopping everywhere in the bottom of the boat, would kill the engine and leave us helpless. I knew now where the water was coming from. Someone had done something to the propeller shaft, and we were taking water through the tube. And it was coming in faster, either that or my pumping was less effective. Very likely both. There was far too much water in the boat now, and if she rolled really badly I did not know whether she would get up again.

Time blurred a lot after that. The boat bumped and wallowed its way through the short angry seas, and the water inside her sloshed about my legs, and all the time I pumped with one hand and steered with the other. It was dark now; too dark to form any sort of judgment of the distance we still had to go. I thought I knew where the island was, but I steered as much as anything by the angle at which the waves came at the boat. She rolled less violently as she got less buoyant, but there was less and less freeboard for her to roll with. And we were losing way. I had a sudden horrified notion that our leeway might take us altogether clear of the eastern end of the island, and that we should simply flounder on southward until she foundered altogether. Then, very nearly ahead, I saw a light. It was slightly on the starboard bow and quite high up. It was a steady, unspectacular, yellow light, and it did not look very far off. I knew what it was, because it could not be anything else. It was the light in my cottage. I was so glad to see it that it did not occur to me to wonder why I could.

I turned the boat towards it, and a moment later she had got her head down and could not get it up again. The water was up to my knees and then in a cold swilling rush up to my waist, and the next thing I knew I was in the water, with nothing but water under me and the waterlogged boat almost on top of me. The engine stopped, and there was nothing to hear but the rolling of the dark water all round and the wallowing of the helpless boat.

I was fully clothed and warm from my pumping, and it took a moment or two for the cold to make itself felt. Then it closed in on my skin with the violence of a sudden physical pressure, so that I felt the air forced out of me through my gaping mouth, and had to fight consciously to pull it back into my lungs again. I put one hand on the gunwale of the boat to steady myself. She had not capsized, but was simply awash, with the waves rolling over her in a small flurry of foam and an inch or two of gunwale standing clear of the surface in between. The stubby mast stood up defiantly, rocking only slightly now with the movement of the water. At least she could not sink, and in my confusion and physical weakness I clung to her with a compulsive instinct of self-preservation.

But she could not get me ashore by herself, and if I did not get ashore within a reasonable time, I should go under, boat or no boat. My thinking mind reasserted itself, and I swung round in the water and looked towards the island. The light still shone. I saw it now reflected on the ridged surface of the dark water in a path of moving yellow segments. It was nearer than I had thought possible, and a sudden spurt of hope flared up in my mind. But I had to make a decision. I had either to use the boat as a sort of life raft until I got closer in to the beach, or leave her altogether and swim for it from where I was. From what I remembered of the way the water was coming ashore, I thought the boat would drift in and come ashore at some point on the north side of the island, but even from here it would take time.

What I did was almost certainly wrong, but it was the decision of a split mind. If I was going to get ashore, I had to exert myself, but I could not find the resolution to let go of the boat altogether. I felt my way hand over hand along the gunwale to the bows. I had left the rope painter coiled down there, and now it was floating about in the wash just inside the boat. I dragged it out until I found the running end of it. I looped it round me under my arms and tied it in what I hoped was a bowline. Then I let go of the boat and struck out in a flat steady breast stroke towards the yellow light.

For a few yards, while the painter ran out from the boat, I swam freely through the dark moving water. Then the line straightened with a jerk and I felt the dead weight of the boat at the other end of it. For a moment I stopped short, kicking defiantly at the water but making no progress at all. Then, gradually but unmistakably, we started to move again. I was swimming at least partly with the drift, and once I had got way on the boat she came more easily than I had expected. Towing a water-logged boat is not the easiest way of swimming ashore after a shipwreck, but it was what I settled for. I had to know she was there, at the other end of the painter. I swam on, ungracefully but steadily and with growing confidence. I do not think this part lasted very long in fact. It suddenly occurred to me that the water was calmer, and then all at once the light ahead went out. I stared blankly into the darkness for a moment, and then almost shouted with relief. The dark hump of the island stood right over me. The light had not gone out; it had gone back over the curve of the slope.

I was in conscious command of the situation now. I even altered course deliberately to bring myself and the boat to the right point of the beach, under the lee of the jetty. Swimming as I was, I banged my knee on the bottom before my hands or feet felt it. Then I crouched for a moment in the shallow water, getting my breath back, until the boat, still lumbering in my wake, grated on the stones just behind me. Then I got up, lifting the loop of the painter off me, and went up the beach. I could not move the boat any further, waterlogged as she was, but there was just enough painter to make fast to the mooring post on the bank. When I had secured her, I went back and groped about in the water inside her stranded bows. My bag was still there, on the bottom of the boat; I did not suppose that total immersion had done my jacket any good, but I was not going to leave it there.

I went slowly up the path, clutching the bag, with the water draining off both of us. The elation of my escape was beginning to die out of me, and I faced the fact that I was back where I had started. I was cold and dead tired and suddenly utterly without hope. The light I had seen was in the kitchen. It had to be, now that I came to think of it, only I didn't think I had left it on. The light was still on in the sitting room, but the curtains were drawn.

I went in at the front door, dropped the sodden bag in the dark hall and opened the sitting-room door. Mrs. Callender was sitting in my chair, with the lamplight on her hair. She got up as I came in. "Where have you been?" she said. "I was getting worried."

CHAPTER 18

It was the sort of thing a suburban wife says to her husband when he has failed to catch the usual train back from the office. There was even the same mixture of emotional implications. There was a note of genuine concern that went with the form of the words, and there were overtones of exasperation and purely self-interested anxiety. It was all grotesquely familiar, only very few suburban wives made the picture Mrs. Callender made as she came towards me with the single lamp burning behind her. And it was not only the 5:50 I had missed.

I do not know what I ought to have done, but I was not in any case in a position to do any very clear thinking. I stood there, cold, wet from head to foot, tired mentally and tired physically, and she came up to me, warm and perfect to every sense, and put her hands on my shoulders. I have thought since that what I did was in fact the prudent thing, but I am not pretending that at the time there was any calculation in it. I wanted to believe that there was a genuine warmth and kindliness in her somewhere, even that she had some kind of regard for me as a person. I did not so much defy the evidence as simply ignore it. I just surrendered and let her take charge of me. It was what I needed and it seemed all I could do.

She said, "Come on, let's get you out of those wet things." She turned me back towards the door and went with me, one hand still across my shoulders, piloting me towards the bathroom at the end of the hall. When we got there, she went ahead of me. She switched on the light, dropped the plug in the bath and turned on both taps. The water came steaming hot. She put a hand on the towels to see if they were dry and spread the bathmat beside the bath. Then she came back to me as I stood in the doorway watching her. "Come on," she said. My soaked clothes clung to me and I fumbled a bit with the cold. We pulled them off between us, and she gathered them up over her arm. My nakedness, when we achieved it, meant nothing to either of us. It was the familiar neutral nakedness of the sick husband when his wife is seeing him through flu. When he is well again, it will mean something, but for the moment it has merely to be dealt with. She said, "Get into that bath." She took the last of my clothes and went out, shutting the door firmly behind her. I still had not said anything, or at least, nothing coherent. I got into the bath.

When I came out of the bathroom, there was a savory smell coming from the kitchen. I do not know why this should have moved me so much, but it did. I was not at all the sort of man, left to myself, to live out of tins. Perhaps that was the trouble. The very fact that feeding myself was to some extent a burden on my thought and time made me suddenly and unexpectedly conscious of the lifting of the burden. But I suppose mainly it was simple association. The smell from the kitchen went with what I needed for the moment to believe. It made that dreadful frozen bundle in the cellar up at the house seem even more improbable than it already did. I went across to the bedroom and put on a dressing gown and slippers. Then I put my head into the kitchen.

The smell of food rolled out at me, and I knew that I was

desperate for it. I was not very clear about it, but I did not think I had eaten anything since breakfast. Mrs. Callender was bending over the stove. She had a tea cloth hitched round her skirt in front as an apron. She turned her head and looked at me over her shoulder. "Warm?" she said.

I said, "Yes, thank you." I did not want to talk to her more than I could help. We had always got on without saying much to each other, and now I instinctively shied off any exchange which might involve more than the immediate physical facts.

She nodded and said, "Sit down, then."

I sat down in my usual place at the kitchen table. There was only one place laid. I said, "Aren't you going to eat anything?"

She seemed to think about this. I didn't think it was the food she was calculating. Then she said, "All right, if you like." She laid another place for herself opposite me. I just sat there watching her. She knew where everything was as well as if it was her own kitchen and she had been there for years.

I said, "Could I have a drink, do you think?"

She shook her head as she put the last things down on the table. "Not yet," she said. "Have some food first. Then by all means."

I did not question this at all. I just nodded, and a moment later she brought over two plates of food and put them on the table. You could call it thin stew or thick soup, as you liked, but it smelled like paradise. She sat down opposite me, and we looked at each other. She was the sort of thing you would have been dizzy with sheer male vanity to have dining with you at wherever the smart place to eat was in London. Then she gave me her quick flicker of smile. "Go on, eat," she said.

I ate all she had given me, and a thick hunk of bread with it. She took my plate to the stove, refilled it and put it down in front of me. Then she brought another hunk of bread and about two fingers of whisky neat in the bottom of a glass. I picked it up and looked at her. "Not you?" I said.

She said, "Not at the moment." She still had some food left on her plate. I drank the whisky carefully, in a series of good-sized sips. Then we both went on eating. She contrived to finish at the same time as I did. I felt warm all through. I could feel the blood pumping round under my skin, so that each part of me was in perfect harmony with every other part. So far as it is given to man to be conscious without thinking, I did not think at all. She got up and took the dirty things to the sink. Then she said, "Bed, then. I want you up at the house in the morning."

I got up and went into the bathroom and cleaned my teeth. I was working perfectly smoothly under fully automatic control. When I went into the bedroom, she was there turning down the bed. I took off my dressing gown, only now my nakedness meant something, to me if not to her. I took hold of her round the waist, and we looked at each other, I in my bedroom slippers and she in her high blouse and dark evening skirt. "You too," I said.

She said, "All right, if you like," exactly as she had when I had asked her to eat with me. I let go of her and got into bed. She turned out the light, which I had not expected, but I could hear her undressing in the darkness. I was warm in the bed before she came to me, but when she came she was as warm as I was.

When I woke up, she was no longer there. The room felt chilly, and there was the beginning of gray daylight outside the window. The wind had gone completely and there was not a sound anywhere. I drifted up out of a sense of warmth and pleasure into a consciousness that I was alone and then, all at once, into a cold, unequivocal awareness of what had happened and where I was. I struggled up into a sitting position and stared round the room. The pieces of furniture put their heads up into the faint suggestion of light from the window, but the floor was all in darkness. There was nothing to be seen in the room but furniture, no clothes over a chair, no oddments on the dressing table. It looked like an unoccupied hotel bedroom that I had got into and slept in by mistake. I was overwhelmed by an appalling sense of isolation. There was nothing of me here but a naked body in a strange bed. All the identifying periphery that made me the person I was was away hundreds of miles to the south, with nothing but a blank in the middle of it. I remembered Mr. Callender saying, "No one knows where you are at all." The air struck cold suddenly on my bare shoulders and back. I shivered violently and plunged back under the bedclothes.

I could not sleep any more, but I lay and waited for daylight. My body at least was warm. I tried not to think too much, because there was very little that thinking could do for me. Later I was wanted up at the house. I didn't know what for, but I should go because there was nowhere else to go and nothing else I could do. Sooner or later someone would tell me something.

When it was lighter I looked over the edge of the bed and saw the toe of one bedroom slipper and my dressing gown in a bundle on the floor by the foot of the bed. I had thrown it across the bed when I took it off, but no doubt it had got knocked off at some point later. There was, after all, as much of mine here as I had gone to bed with. There was nothing of anyone else's. I got up, put on my dressing gown and slippers and went through into the kitchen. My wet clothes had all been disposed round and over the stove, and most of them were dry. The supper things had all been washed up and put away. It was all exactly as I should have left it if I had come back and found the cottage empty. Then I thought, not quite all, because my jacket and town shoes were not there. I went into the hall and looked. The sodden bag was still there against the wall, where I had let it drop when I came in. I opened it, shook out the soaked jacket and put it on a hanger to dry. I put the shoes under the kitchen table. It occurred to me that these were the only things that showed for certain that I had been going for good, and these had not been seen. Or perhaps they had been seen but left deliberately precisely because of what they showed. I had no means of knowing which.

I got dressed in my ordinary working clothes and went down to the jetty. There was gray cloud over the whole sky still, and the water stretched away under it, leaden and almost unruffled. The boat lay as I had left her at the extreme stretch of her painter. The angle of the beach lifted her bow clear of the water, but her transom was well under. The water ran level into her and stood motionless between the emerging gunwales. There was a film of oil from the engine on its surface. Somebody sometime would have to get the engine dried out and started again, but I did not think it would be me. She was no longer my boat.

I went back up to the cottage and got myself some breakfast. I didn't particularly want to eat, but I knew it was the proper thing to do, and managed it quite successfully in an unambitious sort of way. It was now a bit after eight. My watch had done all that the manufacturers claimed for it, and was going steadily despite my swim. Eight was too early to go up to the house, even though I had not been given a time. I had to play at everything's being normal. I still had no real evidence that, so far as the others were concerned, everything was not. I might still find Fifi at the kitchen window washing up the breakfast things and ask her to tell Mrs. Callender that I was there. I did not really think that I should ever see Fifi again, any more than I thought I should ever again use the boat. But I knew too little about anything to be certain.

When I had eaten all I could, I washed up and put everything away. I took the things from over the stove and put them away too. My jacket was still on its hanger on the kitchen door. It would not be dry for a long time yet. I walked round the cottage putting everything into a state of elaborate normality. Every now and then I looked at my watch. At ten to nine I could think of nothing more to do, but I was not going up to the house until nine. I sat down in the sitting-room chair. I wondered how long Mrs. Callender had waited in it the night before and what she had thought about while she was waiting. The one thing I felt reasonably sure of, looking back, was her relief when I came in. I wondered what she had thought might have happened and why she was glad it had not.

When I next looked at my watch, it said more than a minute past nine. I jumped up guiltily, as though I was late for an appointment. I did not look round at anything this time, or go into any of the other rooms. I just went straight out of the front door and up towards the house. When I came over the crest of the slope, I saw all the blank top windows staring down at me in the gray silence, but there was no one about. I walked up on to the terrace and round the side of the house. The kitchen window was empty and I couldn't see anybody inside. I knocked on the side door. For a moment nothing happened. Then I heard a door shut and feet came along the passage. Mrs. Callender opened the door. She was wearing the white duffel coat with dark slacks under it. It was buttoned high to the neck, and the hood was bundled like a high collar round the back of her head. She stood back and nodded. "Good morning," she said. "Come in. There's something I need your help with."

CHAPTER 19

I SUPPOSE the man going to his execution never quite believes, from second to second up to the last, that it is really going to happen to him. I went into the house, despite the white coat, thinking that she might not after all be taking me down to the cellar and the deep freeze. Even when she went ahead of me to the door at the head of the cellar stairs, I still managed to persuade myself that it might simply be a matter of fetching and carrying for her. And yet it was just because I was afraid of what she was leading me to that I was unable to turn aside or refuse to go any further with her. I did not want to be asked what I was afraid of.

There was the same yellow bulb burning in the small space in front of the cellar door, but when Mrs. Callender opened the door, I saw at once that the stairs and cellar were much more brightly lit than they had been. There were no more lights than before, but someone had stepped the power of the bulbs right up, so that the whole place was filled with a garish white light. There were very few shadows, because there was practically nothing to cast a shadow. Where the light struck sideways along the wall, it showed up the rough unevenness of the ancient stonework, but there was not at any point anything between the bulbs and the wall itself. The next thing I saw was that the door of the freezing chamber was standing open, so wide open that it was swung back almost against the wall.

I went down the stone stairs behind Mrs. Callender. Her hair was as I had seen it once before, drawn down tight inside the rough off-white hood of her coat, so that it shone in the white light like burnished metal. Her hands were thrust deep into the big patch pockets of the coat. When we got to the bottom of the stairs, she took one hand out of her pocket and motioned me forward towards the door of the freezing chamber. I did not stop or ask any questions. I was past pretending anything now. I just walked up to the open door and looked inside. The central floor space was empty. The thing I had been getting myself ready to see was no longer there.

I don't know what I may have shown by my expression and behavior all this time, but now I was brought up short. There was an immediate sense of relief, as sharp and sudden as the snapping of a string, but this was only in the front of my mind. Behind it was a hopeless and bottomless apprehension, which seemed almost to hamper my physical movements. I turned my head and looked at Mrs. Callender. She was standing between me and the bottom of the stairs, with both hands sunk once more in the pockets of her coat. She was watching me with an absolute concentration that left no room for any apparent emotion. I looked into her eyes, and for a moment we stared at each other with total mutual incomprehension. Then she said, "Shut the door."

I took my eyes off her only just long enough to put my hand on the handle of the heavy door. I was still looking at her when I swung it shut. Then I looked round again to see to the fastening. I heard myself make some sort of noise. It was between a gasp and a yelp, very undignified and quite involuntary. The thing I had been afraid of seeing had been behind the door. It was there, within a yard of me, propped up at an angle against the outside wall of the freezing chamber, as rigid as a gatepost. Through the wrapping the toes were turned up at an angle to the floor as the thing was tilted back against the wall. I backed away from it step by step until one of my heels kicked over an empty bottle against the wall of the cellar. It knocked down another, and four or five of them went down one after the other, like skittles, jangling on different notes in the brilliantly lit silence. I felt the wall behind me and other bottles against the side of my leg.

Mrs. Callender did not move. She said, "There's nothing to be afraid of. You've only got to be sensible. We had an accident. I need your help. Will you help me?"

I started to answer, but my throat was choked, and all I produced was a sort of croak. I cleared my throat and said, "What do you want?" I did not look at her at all. I was more frightened of her now than I was of the thing against the wall. But I heard her begin to move, and then she walked over and was standing beside the thing just in front of me.

"Come here," she said. I started to move forward, and then she reached up one hand and pulled at the top of the wrapping. A flap of cloth fell away and uncovered the face. The skin was the color of tallow, but it was all perfectly preserved. The mouth was tight shut and drawn down sardonically at the corners. The eyes were closed, but I should have known him anywhere. I was not afraid of him any more. I could not think why I ever had been.

"Jock," I said, "you poor old sod."

"Jock?" said Mrs. Callender. I had almost forgotten she was there. "It's your friend Galbraith, isn't it?"

I turned and walked back towards the wall. "Cover his face," I said. "And lay him down, for God's sake. I can't bear to see him propped up like that."

She flipped the cloth back over the sightless, waxen face. She said, "It is Galbraith, isn't it?"

"Yes," I said, "it's Galbraith. Lay him down."

"We had to know," she said. "We thought it might be, but we had to make certain."

"Galbraith was Mackie?"

"Mackie was Galbraith. We took him on here. We thought he was all right, and we needed someone. He was here for nearly three months." She reached up the same hand and pulled Jock Galbraith's body off balance. She took the weight a bit as it keeled over, but it came down on the flagstones with a thud, and I felt a first sudden spurt of vicious anger. "Nearly three months," she said. She was angry too. "God knows what he may have got hold of."

I felt the bottle against the side of my leg again, and I stooped suddenly and grasped it round the neck. It felt like a hock bottle. It made a good club. When I straightened up, Mrs. Callender was back at the bottom of the stairs. She had both hands out of her pockets now, and her right hand held a gun. The blue-black barrel stuck out as long again as the part she held in her hand, and it had a wide mouth. It was a horrible weapon, not at all the sort of thing women are supposed to carry. She had it pointed at the middle of my body, somewhere about the midriff. It was rock steady. So many people in books and films have guns pointed at them that it has become a familiar experience at second-hand. At first-hand I found it utterly appalling. I wanted above anything to keep her talking. I said, "Was this all you got me up here for?"

"That's right. There were very few people who knew him. I mean very few who were at all accessible. We were lucky with you. Even with you we had to make sure before we used you."

"Sure of what?" I said.

"Sure you would do what we wanted and sure you wouldn't be traced."

I nodded. I had been right to feel that misgiving when Mr.

Callender had said no one knew where I was. I could see no way out now. I said, "Why try to drown me, then?"

"You wouldn't have drowned. But why did you go off like that? Was it something Carrie said?"

"No," I said, "nothing that Carrie said. I just thought it was time to get out."

She shook her head. She did not believe me, but it was no longer a thing she worried about. I had the feeling that she wanted the thing over, and as far as I could see she had only one way of ending it.

I said, "I hope Jock did what he came for. He probably did, you know. You can't tell, can you? Not in your job. I know enough about it to know that. You'll probably never know. But you'll have to assume the worst, won't you? Good old Jock."

She said, "You're not doing yourself any good." And then the side door of the house slammed and there were footsteps upstairs.

She did not move at all, only her eyes widened. Then she called, "George!" She never took her eyes off me or the gun off my midriff. There were more movements upstairs. She called, "George!" again. Something moved at the top of the stairs. I was still watching her, but I saw it over the top of her head. The door had begun to open. It opened a little way and then stayed there. For quite a long time nothing happened. Then the door opened quite slowly and Fifi came to the top of the stairs. She had a knife in her hands. It was an ordinary cook's knife from the kitchen. Mrs. Callender half turned and gave her a quick upward glance. The gun never wavered. Then she moved so that she had her back to the wall and the bottom of the stairs at her left hand. She spoke to Fifi without taking her eyes off me. "How did you get here?" she said. "You've made enough trouble as it is."

Fifi did not answer her. She was looking at me and I looked

back at her. No one had ever looked at me like that before. God knows I did not deserve it. She looked at me, but she spoke to Mrs. Callender. "George is dead," she said. "He never thought I could do what I did. Nor did I. He turned his back on me, and then I did it." She looked down at her hand for a moment, as if she expected still to see blood on it. Then she looked, not at me, but at Mrs. Callender. "George is dead," she said again.

Mrs. Callender said, "That was very wrong, Carrie." She spoke to her as though she was a rebellious child. "You've made nothing but trouble over this. I told you you must be nice to Mr. Giffard. There was no need to fall in love with him."

I knew so little of the relation between them that I did not know, and still do not know, what she was trying to do. Whatever it was, she failed. Fifi looked at me again and gave me her small, secret smile. Then she ran down the stairs and flung herself at Mrs. Callender. She had the knife in her hand, but I do not think she had any real idea what to do with it. I suppose Mrs. Callender must have taken her eyes off me for a split second, but the gun never moved. She reached out with her left hand and caught at Fifi as she came down. I could not see what happened, but Fifi went past her instead of at her, and as she went past Mrs. Callender hit her a short, sharp cuff on the side of her face. The girl went down at her feet, dazed and moaning slightly. She had dropped the knife. Mrs. Callender still faced me with the gun as if we were alone in the cellar. With her eyes still fixed on mine, she reached down and caught Fifi by the hair. She lifted her, still moaning, with her left hand as if she was a rag doll, and pulled her head over her crooked knee. She bent the small head further and further over, until the neck was stretched in a white arc across her dark trouser leg. Then without warning the gun moved. The long barrel swung down like a pole-axe and caught the stretched neck just below the ear. I can still remember the sound it made. I had never heard any sound like it and never wish to hear another. The moaning stopped and the head flopped grotesquely back and sideways as the small soft body slumped to the floor. The gun came up again, but it was the fraction of a second too late. I had already jumped.

My bottle came down across her wrist just before the gun got back to its line. There was a burst of violent noise. The bottle smashed, scattering glass all over the floor. The gun did not go off, but fell with a clatter on the flagstones. There was another, terrible snapping sound mixed with the smashing of glass, and Mrs. Callender gasped and went back against the wall. Then there was a sudden complete silence.

I stepped back until my foot came up against the gun. I stooped quickly and picked it up. I had little more idea how to use it than Fifi had her knife, but I had to keep it away from Mrs. Callender. She still stood, half leaning against the wall, close to the foot of the stairs. Her left hand clutched her smashed right wrist. Her face was chalk white and her eyes were shut. But Jock Galbraith, frozen stiff as a post and trussed up in sacking, lay on one side of her and Fifi, slumped in a still warm bundle, was almost across her feet. If she had been an animal, I would gladly have put a bullet in her, to be rid of her and to put her out of her pain. As it was, I could not, apart from the fact that I did not really know how the damned gun worked.

I went quickly past her and up the stairs. When I got to the top, I turned and looked down. She had not moved or made a sound, but her eyes were open and she was looking up at me. I went out and shut the door behind me. I put the hasp over the staple and locked the padlock over it, but I left the key in the lock. Then I went out into the vast gray silence outside the house.

CHAPTER 20

I TURNED LEFT and went out through the outbuildings at the back of the house. When I was clear of them, I started to run. There was nothing very logical in this. It was still as much as anything the feeling that I had to get away as quick as I could. I also knew that I could not leave Mrs. Callender, whatever she had done, in the cellar and in that company indefinitely; and I had very little idea how long it would take me to establish some sort of contact with the outside world.

I felt the gun bumping against me as I ran. This did not seem very safe. I stopped and took it out of my pocket and looked at it. It fitted nicely to the hand. It was a good weapon so long as you were at the right end of it. After a bit I pointed it into a swell of heather off the path and pulled the trigger. It kicked with surprising strength, but made less noise than I had expected. After a little fiddling with the catch, I pulled the magazine out of the butt. It still had plenty of cartridges in it, and there would be another in the breach by now. It looked for the safety catch, found what must be it and pushed it back. Then I pointed the gun at the heather again and pulled. Nothing happened. I dropped it back into my pocket and started running again.

I ran as far as the powerhouse, and then slowed to a walk. I did not doubt Fifi's belief that George was dead, but there was always the chance that she might have been mistaken. Whatever had happened to it the day before, the boat was now back at the top of the slip. It was locked by a length of chain to a ring set in the rock. I walked along the causeway to the front of the building. The generators were not working, and there was not a sound anywhere. The door was open. There was a key in the inside of the lock with other keys on a ring hanging from it. I opened the door as wide as it would go and went in. There was no one among the machinery in the front part of the house, but the steel door at the back was open. I tiptoed up to it and looked inside. It was not a very large room, but it was full of electronic gear. I was no more judge of these things than I was of the power plant, but it looked to me very formidable. Where George had been sitting, it looked like straight radio, complete and up to now in working order. I did not doubt that, whatever else he did with it, this had been George's link with the outside world, including certainly the red-faced man and very probably Mr. Callender's car. The rest of the room was full of stuff whose purpose I could not even guess at. But it was clearly incomplete. There were even new components standing on their own, waiting to be built into the jigsaw. Not all the packing cases I had carried had been food. As it now was, the radio could not link anyone with anything, nor was George any longer there to be linked.

Fifi had not been mistaken. As she had said, George had turned his back on her. I imagined a first blow which had knocked him forward over his equipment, and then the repeated panic-stricken bashing that looks merciless, but is more likely the result of a desperate determination to put whatever it was out of its pain. I did not think Fifi had been very strong, but the hammer had done well enough without much force behind it. George had been thoroughly broken up and his radio with him.

I went back into the powerhouse. The outboard motor was leaning against the wall on one side of the door. I unscrewed the fuel cap and saw that the tank was three parts full of mixture. I took the bunch of keys from the lock of the open door and went down to the slip. There were only three keys of the right type for the padlock, and the second one opened it. I dragged the boat down the slip and made her fast in the shallow, motionless water at the bottom. Then I went back for the motor. When I was all set to go, I hesitated. I had an urge, now that everything seemed safe and under control, to go back to the cottage and collect my things. But the instinct to get away reasserted itself. Come to that, I might get my things back yet. I was not leaving them with anybody. I pulled the starter cord, and the engine started first time. I headed out southward and then, when I was clear of the rocks, turned east to go round the island. When I was clear of its eastern end, I headed straight for the landing stage on the north shore. The island fell away into the gray emptiness, but after a bit I looked mainly ahead. When I was halfway across, I took my letter to Jock out of my inside pocket. I tore it into small bits and scattered them in the wake of the boat.

When I got to the shore, I made the boat fast to the bottom of the steps and cocked the engine up on its bracket clear of the water. I went up the steps and turned east. There was a car coming over the crest of the road about half a mile away. I had no doubt which car it was. I remembered for the first time the conversation I had had at this place just over forty-eight hours before. It seemed very remote now, but that was when it had been, only the day before yesterday. I looked at my watch. Mr. Callender was dead on time.

There were three possibilities. He might have been in touch, directly or indirectly, with George before Fifi intervened, in which case he would know at least that something unusual was going on. He might have tried to establish contact and failed. Or he might simply not have tried. He had, after all, given me his orders and could expect me there to meet him. I thought I should know when I saw him. I had to see him, because the boat was there by the steps, and in this empty wilderness there was nowhere to hide in the few seconds I had left.

I stood waiting for him on the bank by the tarmac turning circle. I tried to look exactly as if I was waiting to take him back to the island in the usual way, but I was very conscious of the gun in my pocket. If anything, it made me feel slightly guilty. What I did would have to depend on how he looked. I had nothing else to go on. The car came over the near rise and drove straight up to the garage door. For a moment or two he sat at the wheel looking at me. There was no apparent apprehension or hostility in his look, but there was a certain amount of speculation. I thought that probably the second of my three possibilities was the fact: that he had tried to make contact and failed. There was no reason at all why this should have anything to do with me, and there I was, as good as gold, waiting for him as arranged. All the same, I think he wondered. I suppose in his profession you spend a lot of your time wondering.

Then he got out of the car and stood by the side of it. The engine was still turning over quietly. We said good morning simultaneously. He smiled his same slightly turned-in smile, but he was still watching me. I was no good at judging whether a man was armed, but I did not think he could be. There was nothing to suggest it in the elegant lines of his dark suit, and I simply could not see him toting a gun round in a shoulder holster. There might well be some reserve armory in the car. That might be why he had not yet made up his mind to move away from it. But I doubted if he had anything lethal on him. Meanwhile, it was for him to make a move, not me. He had the key of the garage. "All well?" he said.

I managed the right degree of slightly puzzled politeness. I said, "Yes, I think so, thank you." He gave the slightest possible shrug and went over to the garage door, taking his keys out of his pocket. He unlocked the door and swung it up. Then he went back to the car, put her in gear and drove into the garage. I suppose if I had moved quick enough I could have swung the door shut behind him. I do not think, if I had, he could have opened it from the inside, but this is something I still don't know for certain. I moved forward as the idea occurred to me, but before I could get near the door, he was out of the car and facing me. He had the usual briefcase in his hand. That was the only unknown quantity left, but it takes time to open a briefcase and get something out of it. In any case, I did not believe it concealed a weapon any more than I believed his suit did.

He came straight out towards me. Then he reached up and swung the door down. He did it almost without turning round, but I heard the lock click home. He was still looking at me. I think some instinct was working in him, but he had committed himself to a course now, and there was no more hesitation. He said, "Right. Let's go, then." Then at last he turned his back on me and walked up the bank towards the top of the landing stage.

I think he must have known he was perfectly safe. I could no more have shot Mr. Callender in the back there on the landing stage than I could have shot his wife in the cellar. If the question had arisen in his mind, he knew that as well as I did. He stopped suddenly at the top of the bank, and I stopped just behind him. He did not turn round, but spoke over his shoulder. "Why the small boat?" he said.

I said, "The other's taking water."

He knew there was something wrong now, but it was too late

to do anything about it. He walked straight down and got on board. He went to the stern and sat down, facing me along the length of the boat. He had his briefcase on the floorboards by his feet. I went to the painter and untied it. Then I dropped it into the bows and stood back, halfway up the steps. He looked up at me and I looked down at him, and for quite a long time neither of us said anything. There was not a sound anywhere, and the boat did not move an inch from the steps. At last he said, "Well?"

"I'm not coming with you," I said. "Can you work the engine?"

He ignored the question. He said, "Where are you going, then?"

The odd thing was that I really didn't know. "I suppose to the police," I said.

He nodded. "You are armed, I take it?"

I said, "I have your wife's pistol."

"Is she all right?"

"She's hurt but in no danger."

"What about the others?"

"They're both dead."

"Why now?" he said. "What happened?"

"I think I forced her hand."

He nodded again. "It will take you some time to get anywhere," he said.

"I know that. But your radio's not working. You'll have to go over and come back. You'll never find me by then."

"No, I see that." He thought for a moment. "Was Mackie Galbraith?" he said.

"He was, yes. Did you have to kill him?"

He shrugged. He still had the same speculative, quizzical look on his face as he had had when he was talking about the shortcomings of Mr. Hastings. "Well," he said, "I suppose it can be regarded as the usual penalty of failure. My wife found him where he should not have been and shot him in the back. She is apt to be impetuous in such matters."

I said, "I wanted to shoot her just now, but I couldn't. I wonder why?"

He smiled slightly but did not answer the question. Instead he said, "Of course her mistake was shooting him before we had established his identity. Once he was dead, there was nothing to show who he was or what he had been up to. We stripped the place down, but there was nothing at all. He must have been very thorough."

I said, "He was thorough, all right."

"Yes. Anyway, there it was. We knew Galbraith by name, of course, but he was the only one of the probables we didn't know the look of, so we made a provisional identification. But we had to confirm it."

"That was where I came in?"

"That's right. Our people had seen a recent letter of yours. We were lucky, all the same. And we wasted very little time over you. There was very little to waste, of course. Only something seems to have gone wrong. I told you my wife was impetuous in such matters."

"I think she thought Carrie had been talking."

"And had she?"

I hesitated. Fifi was dead now, but I did not know all the ramifications. "Not really, no," I said. "She did—get upset, and that might have put ideas in my head. But in fact it was pure chance. And some degree of carelessness, I'm bound to say. What do you propose to do now?"

"Go," he said. "If Mackie was Galbraith, we should have to go anyhow, I think."

I said, "That being so, perhaps you wouldn't mind telling me what you've been doing here. If I've saved the fort, even by accident, I'd like to know what fort I've been saving."

"I don't see why not," he said. "I have to assume it's already known, in fact. We've been keeping an eye on your American friends over at Inverkyle. They've got a lot of new stuff there—early-warning radar and that sort of thing. You saw the aerials, do you remember? We've been monitoring them a bit. Ultimately we might have jammed them, if the need had arisen. But we were building up our equipment. And now it will all have to go, of course."

I nodded. "I wasn't altogether wrong," I said. "What about you, then? You say you're going. You've got somewhere to go?"

He smiled suddenly, looking at me with something of his old air of quiet amusement. "Ah, indeed," he said. "You can't stop us going any more than I can stop you. The thing's in balance so far as that goes. What will you do? Go back to the Platemakers?"

"Now?"

"Why not now? You've not been gone ten days. They won't have got around to finding anybody else yet." He moved suddenly down the boat, but his hands were empty. He pushed the bows out from the steps, let the engine down and began to wind the starter cord round the flywheel. Then he turned and looked at me again. "You're not really cut out for this sort of thing," he said. "You go along back."

He pulled the cord and the boat moved out with the usual splutter of a starting engine. He turned and set her on course for the island. He did not look back at all. The boat gathered speed quickly and went away steadily into the gray stillness. I watched it until it was hardly worth watching any more. Then I turned and went up the steps. There ought to be something more I could do, but I could not think what it could be. I set out on the long walk home.

P. M. HUBBARD

P. M. Hubbard was born in 1910 and was educated at Oxford University, where he won the Newdigate Prize for English Verse in 1933. From 1934 to 1947 he served in the Indian Civil Service, and upon its disbandment in 1947 he returned to England to work for the British Council in London. He resigned from that job in 1951 to free-lance as a writer, and contributed verse, features and even Parliamentary reports to *Punch*. Later he entered business as deputy director of an industrial organization, but again resigned to earn his living as a writer. Mr. Hubbard's previous novels were *Flush as May*, *Picture of Millie*, *A Hive of Glass*, *The Holm Oaks*, *The Tower* and *The Country of Again*.